"Only a life lived in the service to others is worth living."

- Albert Einstein

DEDICATION
=================

This book is dedicated to the light inside each and every one of us. May reading about this journey remind you of the eternal part of who you are. Regardless of sickness, age, or circumstance, the light inside each of us shall never die.

INTRODUCTION

====================

I am so grateful to be able to invite you on the journey of a lifetime. A tour spanning across the entire United States playing music for people in need. I feel just as lucky to have been a part as I am to have had the privilege to meet and play music for so many courageous and amazing individuals along the way. The original goal of the tour? To visit 50 hospitals in 50 states!

Well - 25, 348 miles later, 51 hospitals, 12 nursing homes, 7 home visits, 3 schools, 3 churches, 1 VA Clinic, 1 Thanksgiving Charity, and to all 50 states... WE DID IT! When I say "WE," I mean every financial donor, Facebook and Instagram friend, hospital staff member, and patient I met along the way. This could have never been done without every single one of you! A total of 78 places I feel so blessed to have visited. I still shake my head in disbelief each time I try to wrap my head around it all.

Instead of chapters, I have divided the book into the 50 states. You will find the states in the order in which I visited them. Each state will include original Facebook and Instagram posts from the road. I have included the original dates and writings in the book, as I want you to feel as if you were on the road with me. To help with this, I have included videos, songs, and news links in the form of "QR codes," - so keep your phone handy to enjoy this interactive portion of the book!

(QR code directions below)

How to scan a "QR code" >

Open the Camera app on your phone as if you were going to take a picture.

Hold your device so that the "QR code" (blue & black square) appears in the center of your picture.

Your device will recognize the "QR code" and show a notification banner at the top of your phone screen when ready.

Tap the notification to open the link (YouTube, Facebook, etc.) associated with the "QR code", and enjoy!! (**First "QR code" is on page 9**)

Thank you for joining me in this book and journey! Welcome to The MUSIC IS MEDICINE TOUR!

TABLE OF CONTENTS

STATE & PAGE NUMBER

====================

MUSIC IS MEDICINE TOUR

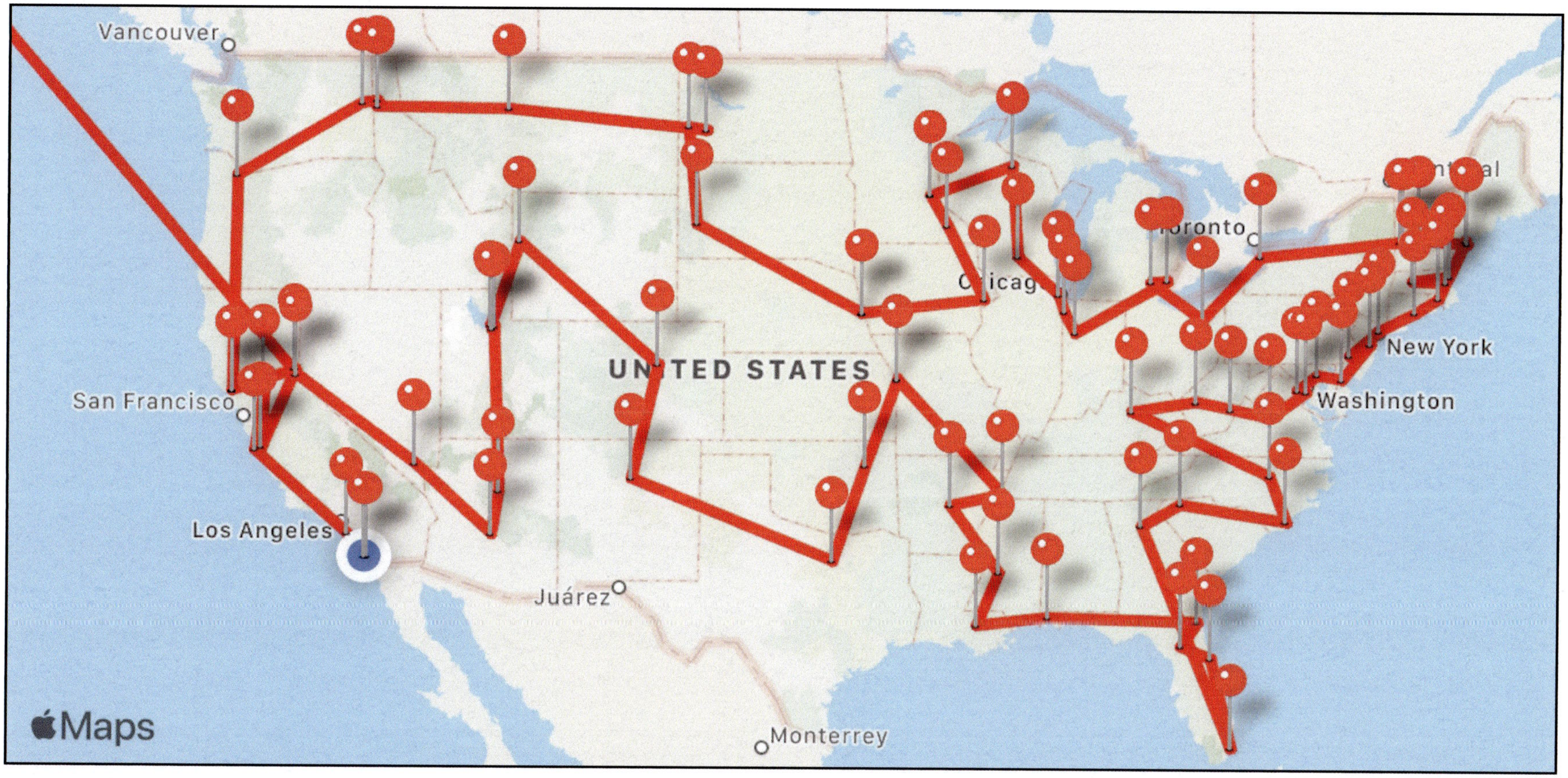

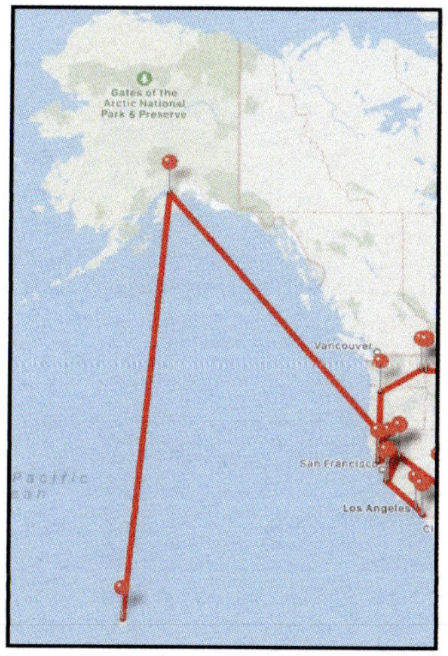

The entire tour, (above) including all 78 hospital stops in all 50 states! Each red dot represents each hospital visited. The plan was to travel in a clockwise loop starting in San Diego, California, (blue dot) and drive through the northern states first.

I ended the tour (small map to the left) flying to Alaska and then finishing in the 50th state, Hawaii!

July 14, 2018

San Diego, CA

Well, it's time to let this journey be known (at least to those of who I haven't crossed paths with recently)... The "Music Is Medicine Hospital Tour"!

I've purchased an ambulance and will be leaving on a 5 month journey across the United States playing music for children and people in hospitals. The goal is to visit at least 1 hospital in every state! (Including Hawaii & Alaska)

The tour will begin in August, and is estimated to take at least 5 months. My hope is to be home by Christmas!

As most of you know, my life has taken on some dramatic changes ever since news of the tumor on my spine 2 1/2 years ago. Physically I feel healthier and more in tune with my body than I ever have before. Career-wise, my musician life has consisted more and more of volunteering at hospitals and singing for those in need. It quickly became obvious to me that there was nothing more important and fulfilling for me to do. Spiritually, I became very aware that there was more to life than just MY wants and worries and that there was something far larger than me at work here. This project, this tour, this journey I'm about to embark on.. is a perfect example of such work.

I'm looking forward to sharing this journey with all of you. More importantly, sharing it with all I have the privilege of meeting and playing music for along the way! FEEL FREE TO SHARE IT with whom you see fit AND WHOM MIGHT BENEFIT FROM IT.

I would absolutely love to visit and meet anyone close to you. The more money raised, the more hospitals I visit! Thank you ahead of time for your support!!

See you all on the road!! MUSIC IS MEDICINE!

#musicismedicine #musicismedicinetour

#HEREWEGO!

QR Code (above) to the original "GoFundMe" video. It was also given to hospitals before visiting as an introduction and explanation of the tour, as well as to raise funds to support the entire tour!

#1 CALIFORNIA

WHERE IT ALL BEGAN

====================

Well, simply put, California is where the foundation for the entire tour was built. I volunteered in my first hospitals, created a video to explain the story and intention behind the tour, launched a GoFundMe page where supporters could donate, and purchased an ambulance that a friend and I spent 4 months converting into a living space for life on the road! It was both humbling and exciting as I had never done anything like this!

The most amazing part of it all, was witnessing the support and momentum that was growing from the beginning. The GoFundMe page raised $30,000 in the first 2 months of it being launched! Hospitals were opening their doors for me to come and volunteer and the "Jambulance" had to have a new engine put in! It was an eventful start to say the least. I started the entire process in April and by September 1st, I was off!

(QR Code) Video of Jambulance build

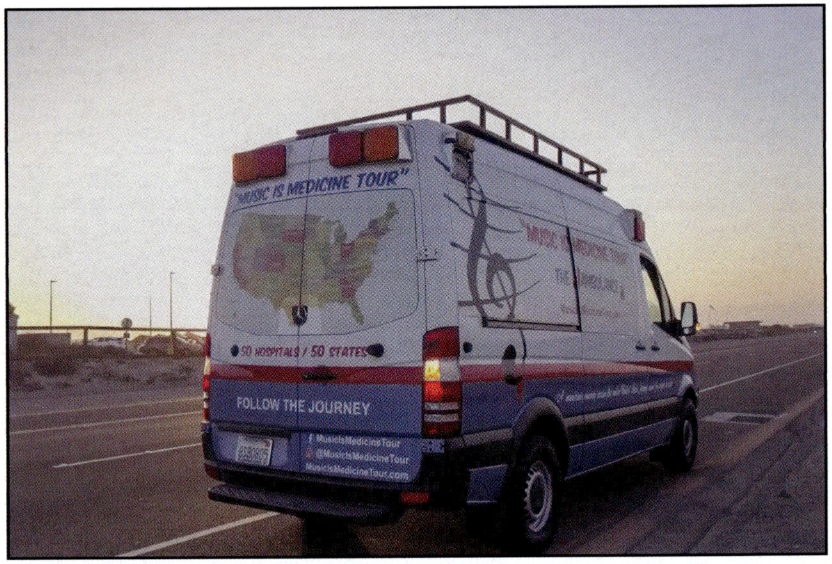

MULTIPLE STOPS

==================

After leaving San Diego, I would make 5 more stops before heading to Oregon. I remember my mom saying, "I'm the last one that wants you to leave, but if you don't get on the road soon, you're never going to be able to go! Winter is right around the corner!"

Although I was gradually making my way north, she was right. I needed to get on the road. In the pages ahead are the 5 stops I made and the Facebook posts that accompany them. Also included is my first "pit stop" to replace the engine!

August 31, 2018

STOP #1: Rady Children's Hospital

San Diego, California

Where the inspiration for this entire tour began, Rady Children's Hospital. This sunrise is for you Layla. My thoughts are with you today @ 9:30am. This brave girl's choice was to dance to "The Macarena" and "Shake It Off" before her surgery today.

#musicismedicinetour #dogood

@musicismedicinetour

September 4, 2018

STOP #2: CHOMP (Community Hospital of the Monterey Peninsula)

Monterey, California

It's not everyday that you find a hospital and environment as giving and open to alternative healing as CHOMP. I've been told to come here by many, as they said I would love it. It is hospitals such as these that will inspire such programs to be created everywhere. Thank you to Angela Coatu and staff for taking me in!

#CHOMP #dogood #musicismedicinetour

September 5, 2018

STOP #3: Witter Ranch Elementary School

Sacramento, California

Wanted to thank Stacy Edelen (@stacyedelen) for having me come to speak and sing to her 4th graders. We had the students write about a gift or a characteristic they each possessed and how they could use it to be of service to others. Their responses were incredible and I feel so lucky to have met all of these amazing children. Here's to planting seeds of inspiration and positive impact at such a young age!

Love you Stace.

#dogood #musicismedicinetour #beofservice

September 20, 2018

PITSTOP #1: Westcoast Sprinter & Auto

Salinas, California

The Jambulance gets a HEART TRANSPLANT! Sorry I've been quiet on the updates lately. We (the Jambulance and I), have been experiencing a little hiccup with engine troubles. Actually, kind of a large hiccup - oil burning and piston rings needing to be replaced has led to needing a completely new engine. Bad news: Pretty costly. Good news: What better time and way to start a 50 state/20,000 mile journey than with a clean slate and new heart/engine! This original 2008 Solano County Ambulance had saved and prolonged the lives of numerous people and families. What a beautiful life it had. I can feel it smiling now, however, as it's NEW HEART is purring and beating strong underneath the hood. Not to mention my own peace of mind, as the last thing I want to worry about is breaking down in the middle of nowhere in winter!

I want to thank "Westcoast Sprinter & Auto" for their expertise, professionalism, honesty, and sacrifice to make this happen. If any of you want to take your Sprinter somewhere, this is the place. I also want to thank the Casey Family, who once again took me in while the Jambulance was on blocks.
Here's to the Ambulance's OLD HEART and the lives it saved. And here's to the "Jambulance's" NEW HEART and the lives it will bring joy and peace to in the future! Cheers everyone. And may the journey continue!!
MUSIC IS MEDICINE.

#musicismedicinetour #hearttransplant #jambulance

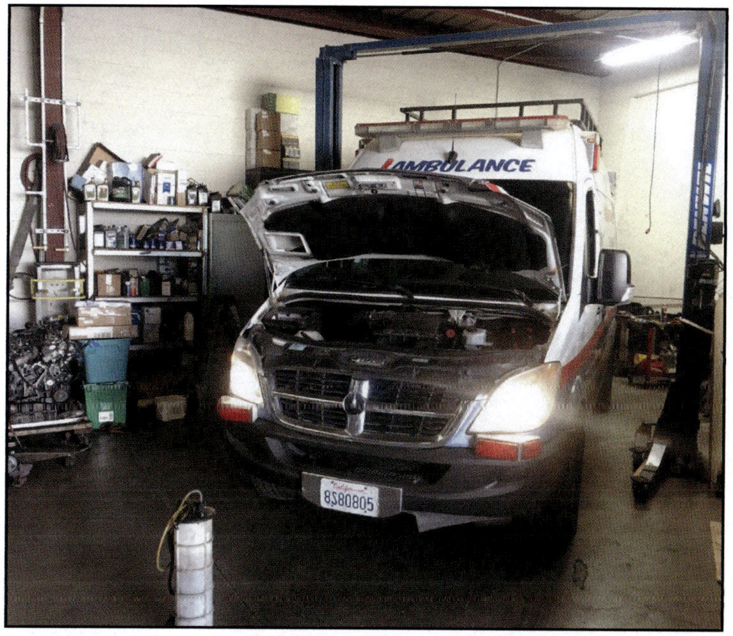

September 24, 2018

STOP #4: Tahoe Forest Extended Care

Truckee, California

I feel blessed to have been given the opportunity to come and play music for the patients at Tahoe Forest Extended Care, where nurses and staff nurture and tend to the needs of elderly in their last years of living. Thank you to Brett Brolliar who has shown impressive courage, dedication, and integrity as supervisor. I am honored and proud to call him my brother! Today blatantly acted as a reminder and sign for me, that the need and desire for connection from elderly people is a necessity to their quality of living, and dying. They all just want to have companionship, period. No matter what level of the aging process they are experiencing (loss of hearing, bed ridden, etc.), they all need connection and someone to talk to. Someone to listen to their stories. Someone to spend time with and validate that they are still alive and worthwhile. To listen to their past. To see them as they still feel "inside." Not just the aging, labeled, hard-to-see-past "outside." This is the secret once again: to see PAST the outside and/or circumstances, and know that there is still the same light inside that was always there. Although a little slower or maybe more dim, it still exists nonetheless. This is how they are still alive. And the less we acknowledge and speak and see them as such, the more dim and lessened it will continue to become. Music, talking, dancing, listening, sharing.. All will BRIGHTEN and enliven this light and truth of who they still are and always have been. It is just as sad, as it is exciting, to know that the opportunity to spend time with these people awaits all of us. Please, if by reading this you are inspired or saddened or moved in any way, drive and/or bring your kids to your nearest senior or elderly home and go sign up to volunteer for one half-hour or hour of your afternoon or Sunday. Go sit and be with a man or woman there who is dying to connect and be heard. I promise, you'll be thankful you did.

#elderlycare #musicismedicinetour #dogood #lightinside

LEAVING HOME

==============

It was time. I had completely finished any last minute touches (build-wise) inside the Jambulance and the new engine seemed to be running great. It was time to make one last stop before heading out of California and into Oregon! Winter and northern states, here I come!

September 29, 2018

STOP #5: Healdsburg Senior Living Community

Healdsburg, California

Picture an entire room filled with 20 seventh graders and 30 senior living residents in a large circle. Each child is teamed up with an elder, given an instrument of choice, and all led in song... This is what you get! Hugs, tears, singing, dancing, and a rare, genuine connection between 2 ends of the age spectrum. I couldn't help but stop in the middle of singing, and point out that this had to be (at least) "close" to the meaning of life! They all agreed. :)
What a great group of kids. So engaged and respectful from the time I arrived. What a special time for me to share my story both as a musician and once again as a teacher. I loved seeing how many questions they had about the Jambulance and the tour. They were all so touched by the entire day!
Here's to inspiring and BEING INSPIRED by young lives.

Thank you once again to Carrie Smith from The Healdsburg School (@thehealdsburgschool) for bringing your students and providing us all with such an incredible opportunity! Thank you to Tony Fisher and the Healdsburg Senior Living Community for hosting and lending me all of your residents for the morning! What a team we were!! Until next time. GOODBYE CALIFORNIA!

#musicismedicinetour #thehealdsburgschool #dogood #kidsinspiration

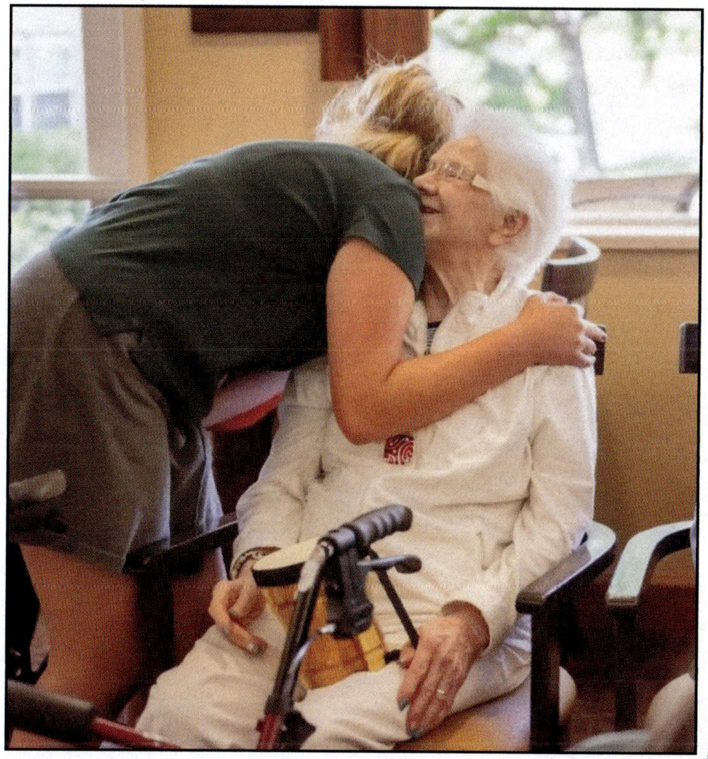

#2 OREGON

A LOT OF FIRSTS

==================

We did it! The Jambulance and I got out of California before the snow started to fall! Oregon had the greenest of scenery. I would pull over numerous times and take pictures of the trees and the streets as I drove through them.

Oregon was also home to a lot of firsts for me. In California, I was able to take advantage of friends and connections I had made both for sleeping arrangements and for hospitals where I could volunteer. In Oregon however, it would be the first time to book a hospital that knew nothing about me or the tour. Who do I ask for when booking a new hospital? Is it different from state to state? How cold was it going to get? Should I base the tour's route on the weather? What if I book a hospital and can't make it due to weather or car trouble?

There was no template for me to follow here, and I learned very early on that I was going to have to let the tour guide and lead me rather than the other way around. In other words, where I was going to visit and the route I was going to take was not in my control. As I will explain throughout this journey, learning to let go was one of the biggest challenges and also one of the greatest rewards.

October 2, 2018

Doernbecher Children's Hospital

Portland, Oregon

I had been told by many about a certain Children's Hospital in Oregon and I can see why. Thank you to Doernbecher Children's Hospital, and "My Music Rx" for allowing me to play and sing with their children and families!! Many egg shakers given out and many new band members! Some sat at the piano with me, others danced. My favorite, however, was the younger of two brothers, whistling through his protective mask while still hooked up to his I.V. Without hesitation, he walked behind me as we brought songs to others throughout the lobby.

It's often hard to paint the picture of these experiences, and most times I am prohibited to take pictures of patients. I hope, however, that you all know this feels like only the beginning of the most beautiful impact I have ever made.

Thank you also to the Fritsch Family for taking me as one of their own, and in helping to make it possible for me to play my first hospital outside of California!

#musicismedicinetour #giveyourgift #musicismedicineforthesoul

#3 WASHINGTON

FAMILY ROOTS

===============

Leaving Oregon, I had reached out to my dad's cousin who lives in Washington. She knew a lot about our family history and taught me things about my dad's side of the family I never knew, including that much of my dad's upbringing was in Spokane! Additionally, there was a Shriners Hospital in Spokane, and the first (among many other Shriners Hospitals in the nation) I was hoping to play for!

October 4, 2018

Spokane, Washington

Wow, what a beautiful little town! It felt like I was in a slightly bigger Lake Tahoe. There was a beautiful river running through it, water falls, and the people were very warm and welcoming. I'm sensing this warmth from people may continue, not only from those in the Pacific Northwest, but for the rest of the states I have yet to see!

I had the opportunity to visit my great grandparents' first house here in Spokane. The picture (upper left) is of them on their wedding day. It was so awesome to surprise my Dad who spent a lot of his upbringing here, and FaceTime him as I was sitting on the front steps of his grandparents' house!

Thank you Washington. You were beautiful, green, and warm-hearted. Thank you also to the Paisley Family for taking me in!

#musicismedicinetour #spokane #family

Enjoy the 1 min QR Code video (above) that Shriners put together of the entire day!

(Unfortunately, if you don't have Facebook you are unable to see this particular video).

October 6, 2018

Shriners Hospital for Children

Spokane, Washington

I couldn't be happier and more impressed than I am with my first experience at a Shriners Hospital for Children. I was greeted with excitement, intrigue, and full trust as they allowed me to not only sing in the lobby for families, but also visit individual rooms to sing and be with the children one on one.

A special thank you to Shay Smith, who not only made the video (below-left), but is a true example of someone who is passionate and talented at what he does. Thank you for opening your doors to such an amazing opportunity, and trusting me with your residents and families. This is what you're meant for buddy!! Congrats.

#shrinershospitalforchildren #giveyourgiftaway #blessed #musicismedicinetour

SEE THE LIGHT BE THE LIGHT

========================

As I was mentally preparing for what I was about to witness, these are the words that came out of my mouth, unannounced, as I exited the Jambulance before entering my first Shriners Hospital for Children...

"**See the light**, **be the light**".

I will never forget it, as the entire tour would be based upon this phrase. I realized in that moment that it was my responsibility to see the "light" in each patient I visited rather than their sickness, age, or circumstance. This eternal part of each of us is what connects us, and what many (especially those I would be visiting in hospitals) may have forgotten. What an honor and what a journey this mantra was about to lead me on. A mantra that would change the course of the tour and my life, forever.

#4 IDAHO

START OF WINTER PREP

=====================

Coeur d'Alene, Idaho, was a lake town I had heard a lot of good things about. The location of it was perfect since I was heading east into Montana next. I wanted to stay as far north as possible so stopping here made the most sense. It was also an important time for me to start gearing up for some colder nights to come. I purchased a couple pair of warm socks, propane for both my "Mr. Heater" and my cooking stove, and a mini fire extinguisher. I also bought a fitness pad which I would use to sleep on that was twice as thick as my current yoga mat. Walmart would soon become my second home, as I would purchase almost anything I needed as well as sleep in their 24 hour parking lots.

October 8, 2018

Kootenai Health, Rehabilitation Hospital of the Northwest

Coeur d'Alene, Idaho

So lucky to have been able to play at 2 such amazing hospitals. Kootenai Health - so many had told me about. Rehab of the NorthWest - I called out of the blue. Such a special opportunity, playing for 25 residents all in wheel chairs recovering from a range of surgeries. My story was especially impactful and encouraging for them. Thank you Jennie Pipoly for opening your doors to me, and giving me such an intimate opportunity to connect with your residents. Coeur d'Alene! What a beautiful place!

#kootenaihealth #rehabhospitalnorthwest #musicismedicinetour

#5 MONTANA

GREAT FALLS, MONTANA

=====================

Before leaving Coeur d'Alene, I received an Instagram message from a news reporter named Katie Tercek in Great Falls, Montana. I had never been, nor did I have any intention to visit. She sounded very interested, however, in doing a story on the tour and explained how special it would be if I visited. Located in the middle of Montana and on the way to North Dakota, I figured it was meant to be and told her I'd be honored!

Benefis
HEALTH SYSTEM

October 17, 2018

Benefis Health System

Great Falls, Montana

What a privilege and surprise to be featured on ABC Fox News in Great Falls, Montana! Thank you to Katie Tercek, who's enthusiasm, passion, and professionalism brought me to Great Falls in the first place. You're such a go-getter! Thank you also for recommending Benefis Health System as a place to visit and play.

As far as the Benefis Health System staff - Becky Pugh (Community Mentor), Sariah (Long-term care), and Peter Gray (Executive Director). You guys took me in like family and treated me like one of your own. Peter invited me to spend the night with his family, gave me a home cooked meal, a shower, and sent me on my way. You guys couldn't have given the Music Is Medicine Tour a better experience. Thank you all so much! Until next time!!

#benefishealthsystem #greatfallsmontana #musicismedicine #grateful

SNOW ALREADY?!

===============

My last morning in Montana, I woke up to unexpected snow covering the Jambulance. It was only October, so this came as a surprise to me. My goal was to make it to Maine and then start heading south before Christmas, so it was time not only to map out an approximate route, but become more aware of possible storms and weather patterns. Inside the Jambulance, I put up a map (middle-right), and used yarn and pins to detail an approximate route, order of states, and towns to visit. I also stuck my first guitar stickers on the back of the rear window map of the Jambulance! I was 4 states in, and was ready to finish my drive across this big sky before it snowed any more on me! .. Alright 6 hour drive to the border of North Dakota - here I come!

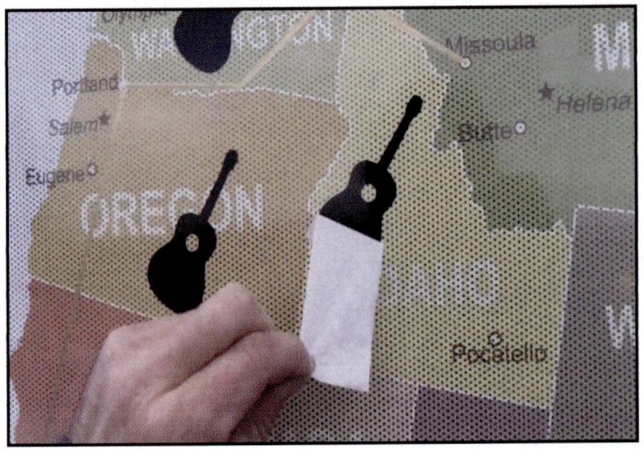

October 19, 2018

Missoula, Montana

Thank you Montana. Your mountains were snow-capped and beautiful. Your people were inviting and warm. You surprised the Jambulance and me with your welcoming of white winter! Here's to the BIG SKY country!!

#bigskycountry #jambulance #winteriscoming

#musicismedicinetour

#6 NORTH DAKOTA

COLD NIGHTS

==============

Although I had experienced my first snow in Montana, I had slept in a warm house! My first night in Dickinson, North Dakota, however, the weather at night was set to be 15 degrees with a 5 degree wind-chill factor and I had no warm house to sleep in. Thank you to a friend in San Diego who located a Walmart near me and surprised me by ordering me my first 'zero degree' sleeping bag! I also bought a fleece mask to cover my face. I remember lying in bed in the Jambulance, listening to the wind. It lightly shook the van and created a whistling sound as it passed over the metal roof rack. I smiled as it shook and sang me to sleep. I also smiled because despite the howling wind, I was warm.

GOOD OL' BOYS

================

The cold nights were balanced out with the inviting conversation and genuine nature of North Dakota's people. I'll never forget sitting in a restaurant and talking with a gentleman for 45 minutes over breakfast, as if there was nothing more important than the conversation at hand. I've never felt a stranger so comfortable and genuinely interested in talking. I could have sat with him the entire day. What was more impressive is that he, a ranch owner, could have done the same.

October 20, 2018

CHI St. Alexis Health

Dickinson, North Dakota

Thank you to Renee and the welcoming staff of CHI St. Alexis Health in Dickinson, North Dakota, who invited music into their hospital for the first time!! Thank you for trusting me to sing and bring joy to your patients in the Kidney Dialysis wing. A highlight was handing one of the nurses an egg shaker, prompting her to dance, and the "out loud" laughter from a gentleman whom the nurses said had not smiled or laughed in the 2 years he had been there! So good. Thank you also for welcoming me into the numerous rooms to meet and play for your residents and patients. My favorite part, was you sharing with me the impact it had on your residents and that you are planning on reaching out to local musicians to do this more often!! This is one of the many hopes of this tour - to inspire hospitals, other musicians, and artists of all kinds to realize they too can be a part of bringing joy and healing to those in need.

#musicismedicine #musicismedicinetour #allcanheal #dickinson

#7 SOUTH DAKOTA

October 23, 2018

Somewhere in South Dakota

In 4th grade I wrote my State Report on North Dakota. Maybe I knew more then, than I had given myself credit for. Apparently it was meant to be. Having just spent the last week in North & South Dakota, I can tell you I've never been so touched by a state or part of the country. Although chilled by the evening winds, the experience warmed my spirit.

Theodore Roosevelt's passion and experience of living in North Dakota for as long as he had, influenced me and spurred my curiosity. His conservation efforts only fueled me to want to explore more. The badlands of Medora, the prairies of Belfield, and the Black Hills of Deadwood, Keystone and Crazy Horse - they all took a piece of my heart. The clash of the Native Americans and the Ranchers of Manifest Destiny took place so prominently, that I could feel it. I could feel the history here.

I found myself watching videos, visiting book stores, and reading more and more about it. I could see the huge herds of bison for as far as the eye could see. I could hear the calls of the Native Americans as they rode their horses through the creeks. And then, in a blink of an eye... GONE.

In place now - ranches, small restaurants, and gas stations,

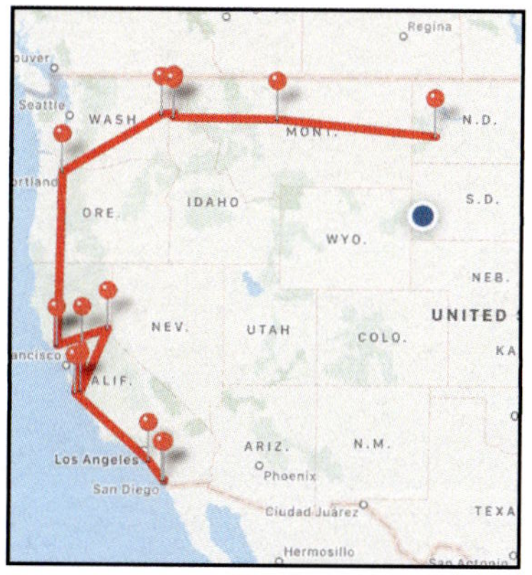

sparsely scattered across the plains filled with polite, simple people, and warm-skillet meals. Locals and small town residents having conversation because that's just what you do here. Treat each other and those that cross your path with respect, honesty, and a genuine nature. The same respect ironically that I felt they had for the Native Americans. As if there was a unique combination of the past combined with the respect for their own modern-day culture and what they stand for now.

I am left with tears of the past, but true appreciation for its culture and what it stands for today. I will come back to you North and South Dakota. Like Theodore, you touched my heart.

#nativeamericanhistory #loveyounorthdakota

October 24, 2018

Rapid City Regional Health

Rapid City, South Dakota

How awesome it was for Rapid City Regional to open the doors for me to their patients. I was able to sing in the front lobby waiting room for families awaiting their appointments, and was escorted into 3 different wings of the hospital to visit individual rooms and treatment centers. Thank you also to Rapid City Regional Health for featuring the Music Is Medicine Tour in such a great article! (below)

#rapidcityregional #lobbylove #musicismedicine

(QR Code above) Rapid City Regional article

#8 NEBRASKA

CARHENGE?!

===========

I began my journey in Nebraska not knowing what to do or where to visit, but would soon come to appreciate the Cornhusker State as one of the most enjoyable and meaningful states of all! Upon leaving North Dakota, I called a friend of mine who helped me not just with hospitals that I could visit, but with interesting landmarks and sites that each state was known for. She mentioned a place called “Carhenge” in Nebraska, a formation that was built as a replica of “Stonehenge” in England except made out of cars! What an amazing site. Humorous, yet impressive. Free of charge to visit, and found literally in the middle of nowhere.

A WHOLE NEW WORLD

===================

While driving through Nebraska, I stopped to get gas somewhere in between Alliance and Omaha. It was late at night and I walked inside to get a snack. As I entered, I noticed there were more people inside than normal. There was a plethora of books on disc, a full restaurant, a mini movie theatre, and a place to get a haircut?! I was totally confused, and as I walked further toward the back, there was a sign for “SHOWERS.” Alright, I thought, where am I? It felt almost like a mini-casino and it was apparently the place to be while in the 'middle of nowhere' Nebraska.

Up to this point, (8 states into the tour), I had been sleeping mainly in Walmart parking lots. Little did I know, there was an entirely different world and a community of “TRUCK STOPS!” As I sat to eat, a trucker there taught me all about the lifestyle, the hours they drive, where they stop along the way, and most importantly how to receive a token so that I could shower! Thank you, TA truck stops. You showed me a different way of life, a sub-culture of hard-working men and women, and a safe place to sleep protected from the wind by tall trucks.

October 26, 2018

Boys Town National Research Hospital

Boys Town, Nebraska

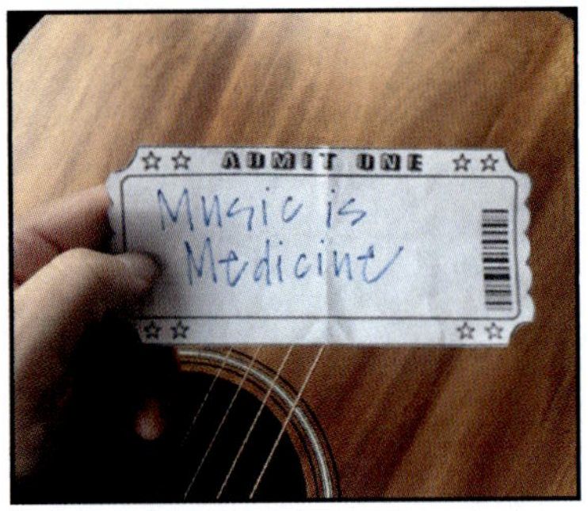

How to put into words the daily experiences of this tour is nearly impossible. Today I was called in the morning and asked if I was able to come and sing for a 9 year old boy who was going in for surgery at noon. Aside from just waking up and it being 50 miles north of my original route, I knew I was supposed to be there. I agreed and got ready as quickly and calmly as I could.

On my drive, my smile grew larger with each mile driven. As if the farther I went, the more wealthy in the "life tank" I became. There was nothing else and no where else I would rather be in the entire world than in this situation. Right now. Driving from Lincoln to Omaha, Nebraska, to visit a young boy before surgery to learn and sing him his favorite song. "Long Cool Woman In A Black Dress" by the Hollies was his request. It was apparently his grandpa's favorite song and he had taught it to him.

I quickly learned the song before walking in, and before I could give him a high-five he immediately reached out to give me something. It was a $5 bill, and an ADMIT-ONE paper ticket. He says to me, "This is for the Music Is Medicine Concert, and I've already got my ticket." His mother, grandmother, nurses, staff, and myself all burst into laughter. I shook my head, took the ticket, gave the $5 back to his mom behind my back and said, "Well, your concert has arrived. I'm glad you bought a ticket and I have a present for you as well." I handed him an egg shaker and a guitar pick. "I am learning how to PLAY guitar!" he said. " This is perfect! And red, yes. This is my favorite color. Perfect!"

As I started to play his favorite song, you could tell he was going through some pain. He looked down and grimaced. I looked at the nurses for permission to continue and they all nodded yes.

I will never forget the chorus. He looks up, eyes closed, and starts bobbing his head. Up and down up and down. He didn't stop until the end of the song. Smile across his face, longer than his cheeks. He opens his eyes and says, "That was it. That was the song. You did it." I smiled back at him proudly, nodded and said, "I did. And I learned it for you."

Again, there's no more wealth in the world, than when you fill someone's tank by being yourself. And in this, they fill yours.

Thank you Natalie, Becky, and the rest of the staff at Boys Town National Research Hospital for calling me in today for a pre-surgery boost! For letting me sing my first infant to sleep! And for joining in to sing before leaving with the entire nursing staff with egg shakers in the lobby! So awesome. All of it.

#musicismedicine #admitone #lifewealth

A PROUD MOMENT

==================

I'll never forget eating lunch with the Jambulance door open and my feet hanging out over the edge, looking out over the cornfields of Nebraska. I had just received an email from the hospital telling me what an impact the visit had made on Caleb and his family, as well as thanking me for what a huge difference the music made on their day as an entire staff. Around the same time, I received a text from my mom telling me how proud she was of me for what I was doing.

For the first time in my life, I had become a witness to it. In other words, I was able to see my own life and liked what I saw more than I ever had before. Here I was, eating lunch in the cornfields of Nebraska feeling more than ever, that my actions were making a difference in the lives of others. This was only the beginning of one of the greatest rewards of the tour - becoming proud of myself and what my life now stood for.

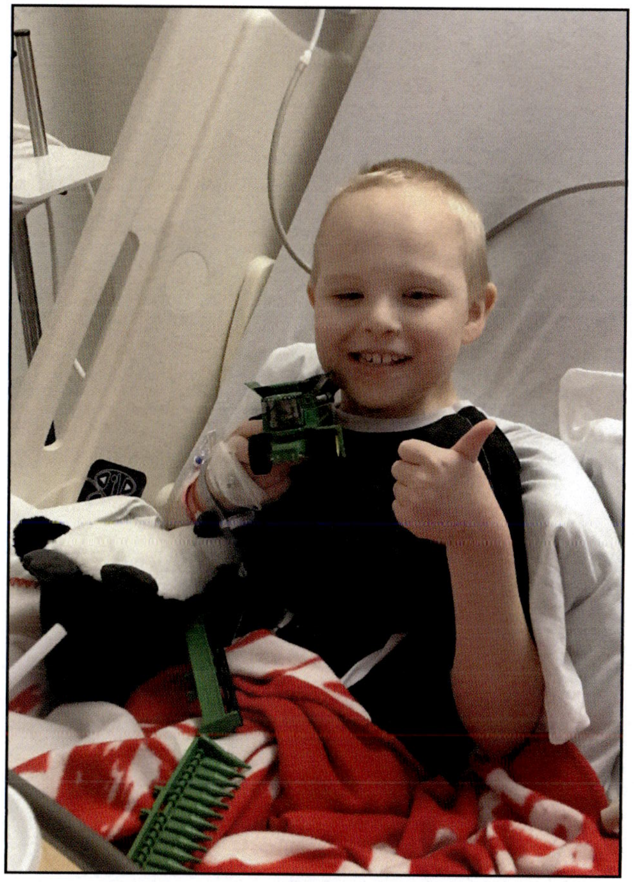

Caleb after his surgery. Thumbs up! Everything went great!

#9 IOWA

AN INSPIRING TRADITION

======================

Months before the tour started, someone had told me about a tradition in Iowa that won my heart over. It was a tradition that occurs at every Iowa Hawkeyes home college football game. The tradition is exactly what inspired me to reach out to the University of Iowa Hospital in the first place and come play music for its children and its patients. Enjoy, as the video below explains all.

(QR Code above)
Hawkeye home game tradition.

October 29, 2018

University of Iowa

Stead Family Children's Hospital & Clinics

Iowa City, Iowa

Thank you to Mark Bernat and the "Project Art" Department at the University of Iowa Hospital & Clinics. They opened the beautiful atrium in the front of the hospital for me, rolled out the baby grand piano, and gave me the floor. Empty when I started, within minutes people started to come in and sit and enjoy. My favorites were the patients who couldn't leave their beds that were brought out to the atrium, nurses by their sides, smiling as they came out to listen. As I looked up, I waved and sang to the patients (IVs still attached), with their parents and family members on the upper floors, standing at the railings listening and watching from above. Before long, there was a soothing mini-concert being enjoyed by all. From playing music at bars, restaurants, and weddings to this... I wouldn't trade it for the world.

By the third song, a little girl and her mother walked out and sat in the front row. I stopped, offered her an egg shaker and asked if she wanted to join. For the next hour, she and I sang, danced, and brought laughter to all. I wish you all could have witnessed the scene. "You're now in a band my dear," I said to her as we bowed to the crowd.

*As I finished, I walked around to meet all that came out to enjoy the music. The one that touched me the most, was a gentleman who had been rolled out of his room in his hospital bed. He was awaiting a liver transplant. I couldn't help but notice the color of his skin. It was so yellow, that when I walked up to him you could feel the room stop as if shocked that I would approach him. As I reached out my hand to shake his, the first words out of his mouth were, "How many '**I knows**' are in that song?" The song he was referring to, was "Ain't No Sunshine" by Bill Withers. We all laughed out loud, as the question broke all tension that was present in the room. I started counting as I pretended to sing again - "Twenty seven." I said to him with a grin as the room burst into laughter.*

As I'm packing up to leave, my new bandmate (below) walks up to me and says, "If we're in a band together now, does that mean you're coming to lunch with us?" Her mom and I both laughed.

(I think you all know my answer).

#wouldntbeanywhereelseintheworld #musicismedicine

LONG DISTANCE MEDICINE

========================

After leaving the hospital, I was called and asked by a close friend to see if it was possible to play music for a young girl named Adeline. She had been diagnosed with Acute Lymphoblastic Leukemia and was in the hospital and in critical condition. The only issue was that she was in North Carolina. Visiting and even FaceTiming her was not going to be possible. I decided to record a video and a song and sent it to her. This would become a blessing, as I soon realized that the Jambulance and I didn't necessarily have to be (physically) present in order to bring music and joy someone's way. (Long-distance) musical medicine was now born! From this point on, I could and would sing to anyone who needed a song no matter how far away I was.

Adeline, "long-distance musical medicine" is and will forever be dedicated to you and in your memory. The amount of compassion and kindness you inspired in so many in such a short time is an absolute blessing. Your family and friends love you. May the memory of you always be safe in this book, and your spirit live on in your story.

IT'S ABOUT THE JOURNEY, NOT THE DESTINATION

==

After leaving the hospital and about 3/4 the way across the state of Iowa, the Jambulance had broken down. Luckily, I was able to roll into a gas station, but to make matters worse, the rain came pouring down. Literally. The fix for the leak in my windshield that I thought I had taped and caulked properly, obviously hadn't worked. Water was dripping inside the cab and running down the inside of the windshield and onto the dash. I couldn't get out to fix it, and I couldn't move the Jambulance to get under an over-hang. I remember thinking, "This is one of those moments." It was black or white. I was either going to start to cry and clinch my fists and scream, or laugh my butt off realizing this very well could be one of the funniest stories to tell - especially if I made it through!

Luckily I chose the latter. I started shaking my head, laughing, and saying out loud to myself, "Of course! Of course it would start raining and leaking inside when I'm broken down on the side of the road in the middle of Iowa at night!!"

Nine states in, over forty tanks of gas, and nearly 4,500 miles... GREEN PUMP = DIESEL. I knew this! Well, apparently not in Iowa, and apparently not at BP gas stations. I had put UNLEADED GASOLINE into my DIESEL ONLY engine.

All said and done, I was picked up the next morning by a father and son duo whose job was working on diesels only. I was in the right hands. The father turns to me while we're riding to his shop with the Jambulance in tow and says, "Sorry to tell ya, but I make a lot of money off you western-state folk comin' out here thinkin' diesel is green. I tow folks all the time, make the same mistake as you. They change the pumps around here. Ya gotta keep a close eye on 'em!"

The infamous GREEN pump

$400 later, Arby's "all-beef" sandwiches shared with the mechanic crew, and I was back on the road. We all make mistakes. I figure why only share with a chosen few, when I can put it in a book and laugh about it always? As my mom once told me, "Life's about the journey, not the destination." Ain't THAT the truth!

#10 MINNESOTA

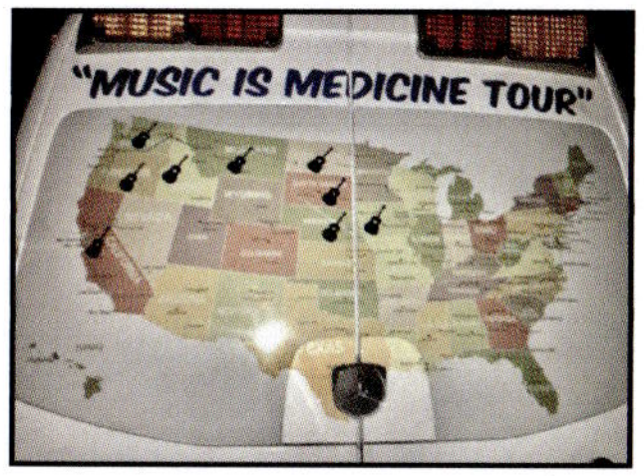

MINNESOOOOOOO - TA

====================

I had one main goal before visiting Minnesota, and that was to play music for the patients at Mayo Clinic. I had heard such amazing things about it, including that it was one of the top hospitals in the country. Upon arriving to Minneapolis however, I quickly realized there was another priority that was going to have to be taken above all else - to gear up for the winter in the northern states of the mid-west! This was going to be a different kind of cold. Although I had toughed-out the cold of the Dakotas, it was later in the fall now. The first night in Minneapolis was 14 degrees, and I accidentally left the passenger side window open. I might as well have slept on the roof! The second night was 7 degrees. The third night, 3 degrees. Luckily, I had learned prior to getting to Minnesota that the REI headquarters was in Bloomington, just south of Minneapolis. Thank you again to a team of friends who told me to get my rear in there and purchase what I needed. Boots, a (real) zero degree sleeping bag, gloves, down jacket, reflective sleeping pad, long johns, sleeping bag insert, and 2 Nalgene bottles. I had learned from watching videos of people climbing Mt. Everest, that putting boiling water in Nalgene bottles was the best way to keep your sleeping bag warm. I would place them at the top and bottom of my sleeping bag before bed and drink them throughout the night if I got cold. I learned quickly that the key to a good night's rest was keeping my core warm throughout the night.

I laughed when I awoke to see the water, frozen, dripping out of the Jambulance sink! Eggs, all food in the cooler, any water or liquid - hard as a rock.

LONELINESS

=============

During the second day, I decided to check out the Mall of America. It was nice to be around people, watch a movie, and honestly feel like a normal person again doing normal things. Little did I know it would come crashing down as I left.

Walking out of the mall and after spending a full day inside, I remember feeling an empty feeling in my stomach as I walked toward the doors. I watched everyone leave with their family and friends, get into their cars, and drive home. Back to their warm houses, warm beds, and daily lives. What was MY "daily life"? Oh yah - sleeping in a van, no permanent home, and in Walmart parking lots! I remember watching everyone leave as the mall was closing, realizing I was the last one there. I could see the Jambulance far off in the parking lot, alone, and I didn't want to be in it. I didn't want to freeze another night. I didn't want to be alone. I doubted for the first time wanting to be a part of such a crazy journey. I just wanted to be and feel normal. I had to ask myself for the first time since leaving, "Why was I doing this again?"

Thank you to a couple friends, who when we talked, helped me remember what I was doing, why I was doing it, and that this too shall pass. One of them also told me that this was a perfect reason and night to get a hotel. She was completely right, and when I checked in to get a room, I had never felt so relieved and rejuvenated. I've never loved the company of others in the same building and a warm bed to myself so much. I am a positive person, and have never been so motivated by a mission in my life. However, everyone's armor cracks at some point, and this was my time to mend.

Me, having just ordered take-out food, under the covers watching the 49ers game. Happy, warm boy again :)

November 9, 2018

Mayo Clinic

Rochester, Minnesota

What an honor to have had the opportunity to play at the "Mayo Clinic" Hospital today in Rochester, Minnesota. Up until today, I had heard nothing but amazing things about this place and they did not disappoint. Of all the hospitals I've played in and visited thus far, I've never felt so much professionalism, care, and cleanliness in an establishment. Every time I turned a corner, it seemed like there was a piano in a new, bright atrium that I hadn't seen before. Each piano was open to be played by anyone who wanted, providing the hospital with the joy of music throughout nearly the entire facility. Guided tours, free 30 minute "Wellness Sessions," a museum dedicated to veterans, and a Cancer Education Center were among the highlights that I caught.

It felt like the entire experience in Mayo lifted your spirit. As if anyone who walked in there (patient, visiting family member, or employee), would leave better than when they first came. So much light. So much music. So much passion.

Thank you to Sarah Mensent from the Mayo "Center for Humanities and Medicine" for allowing me to play piano in the front of the hospital in the beautiful Landow Atrium, where the entire hospital and it's patrons walked through. I have to admit, it's the most nervous I have been to play in any hospital thus far. What an honor. What a privilege.

Thank you also to Stefan Garr, for his dedication and advice on music as a fellow pianist. Stefan is a volunteer musician there, and treats the hospital to his classically trained and unique sound on a weekly basis. Your passion is admired my friend. May we all learn from a place such as this. And in times of hurt, distress, or sorrow, may we let unfortunate occurrences be only an incentive for us to do more good.

#musicismedicine #dogood #healing

Shriners Healthcare for Children™ — Twin Cities

2 HOSPITAL VISITS

==================

My goal was to play in at least one hospital in every state, but given my relationship with Shriners, I was committed to playing at any Shriners that would welcome me. Plus, I was headed to northern Wisconsin and it was on my way. So, I headed up to Twin Cities and my second Shriners Hospital!

November 12, 2018

Shriners Children's Hospital

Twin Cities, Minnesota

I've never witnessed such an enthusiastic and engaging staff as when I played music for Shriners Children's Hospital in Twin Cities, Minnesota. Shout out to all of them, who were not only welcoming to me but made anyone who entered laugh and feel more upbeat than when they first came. After rolling their upright piano down the hall and into the main atrium for me, the staff all came out of their offices and joined me in singing and dancing. No joke. Every single one of them.

Afterwards, as we are all laughing about what had just transpired, they insisted that I be decorated in Shriners garb. A hat, 2 shirts, sweatshirt, and a blanket that one of them took out of her office, concerned that I stay warm. "Welcome to an example of Minnesooota-nice," she said as she smiled and handed me the blanket, making fun of her own accent.

Thank you ladies (pictured right). You not only brought me joy and laughter, but I know you do the same for any child who enters your little "hospital happy-land!" So good for so many.

#whatateam #shrinerstwincities #musicismedicinetour

YOU JUST NEVER KNOW

====================

To try and put into words the last children's room I entered would be impossible. Picture two young boys, both extremely quiet and shy. They've both been waiting in their hospital room for me to come and play them a song. When I arrive, I can tell they're excited but each is afraid to make eye contact or look up. I asked their mother what kind of music they like, and she tells me anything by Michael Jackson. What happened next, was priceless. The boy in blue (pictured lower right) jumps up and suddenly breaks out in a dance, robot-style. The same boy who hadn't been able to look up for fear of making eye contact, was now performing dance moves as if he were Michael Jackson's counterpart. His mom threw up her arms and we both laughed. Needless to say, I played the entire song with some added verses.

Both the brothers holding their blue & red egg shakers.
Notice how proud our little dancer is. (right)

#11 WISCONSIN

COLD WEATHER / WARM HOME

=============================

Thank you to the Pride family for letting me stay at their beautiful house on one of the many gorgeous lakes in Minocqua, Wisconsin! On the coldest night of the tour, I was cozy in a warm bed accompanied by 3 cats. :)

Thank you also to Keth (cool name, huh?) and Katie for letting me crash in yet another warm home just south, in Madison, Wisconsin! I walked through the University of Wisconsin campus and loved the town of Madison. The town, nestled in between 3 lakes, had an upbeat, college town feel to it. My favorite part, however, was being able to watch the Packer game at the Pride household and eat original melted cheese curds! Love you guys!!

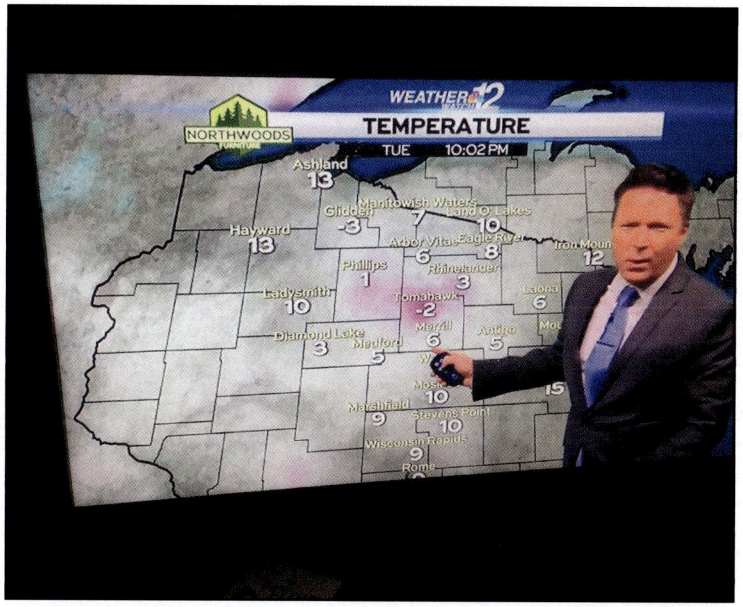

November 15, 2018

UW Health University Hospital

Madison, Wisconsin

Well today was a first for me, as well as for the UW Health University Hospital. Mandy Kron, Art Coordinator of the hospital, had taken me to 5 different spots to play music - the operation waiting room, the cafeteria, cancer center, and two different atriums. All of which went great. None however would bring quite the laughter and enjoyment as the 6th location she brought me.

As I finished playing my last song in one of the atriums, a staff member in a cart pulled up. He stopped right in front of me and asked, "You want to make some mobile- music?" I looked at Mandy as I wasn't sure how to react. "You mean," she asked, "for Ryan to join you in the cart and play music? Do you plan to drive around with him!?"

"Well, yah. That was my thought," he answered, as if maybe he was overstepping his ground. Mandy shrugged her shoulders and looked at me. I could tell she didn't want to commit me to something if I didn't want to, as well as me needing to be on board if we were going to do something like this. I could tell immediately this wasn't anything that had been done before.

"I'm game." I responded with a laugh. "What an awesome idea. I think it could bring a lot of happiness to a lot of people, no?" We all smiled at each other and agreed. "Let's do this!" the mobile cart-man said as he cleared the back seat for me to sit.

For the next 15 minutes, my musical driver and I drove through hallways, atriums, waiting rooms, cafeterias, lounges, elevator lobbies, staff offices, and just about anywhere we could fit the cart. Everyone we drove past had the same reaction we did - Really? Is that music coming down the hall toward us? Is the driver really playing an egg shaker? Rarely have I seen that much laughter and pleasant surprise in a hospital setting, including Mandy following us with her camera waving at people and laughing as we continued on.

Thank you to UW Health University Hospital for making this a stop for the tour. Thank you to Mandy Kron for all the amazing art and music she brings to this environment. And thank you to my private mobile-music driver, Ken!! You made everyone's day man. There'll never be another first like that again!

#laughterismedicine #mobilemusiccart

UNEXPECTED FLIGHT HOME

=======================

Upon driving into Chicago, I learned of one of my best friends in northern California needed surgery to remove a tumor from his brain. I knew I wanted to be there and remember calling my brother for advice. “This is all part of the tour,” my brother said. “There’s no assigned route. Musical Medicine goes on a plane now and back to California!”

I was able to leave the Jambulance at a friend’s house in Chicago and hopped on a plane the next day. I made it in time to be with my friend and his family the night before, as well as the day of his surgery.

TEAM SCOTTY - night before the surgery. (Pleasanton, California)

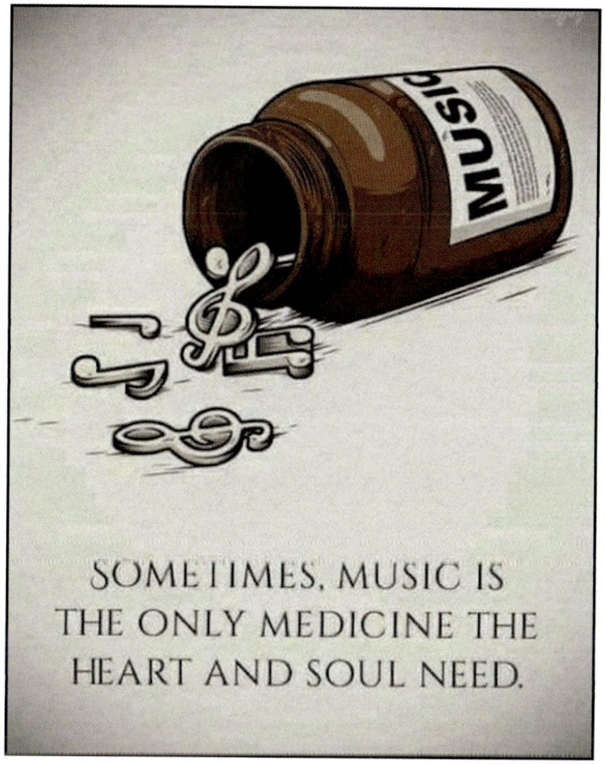

#12 ILLINOIS

BACK TO THE MID-WEST!!

=====================

When I returned back to Chicago, it was pouring rain. I walked the downtown streets, visited the local zoo, and went to a play, "Ms. Saigon." Thank you to my good friend Wendi Williams, for hosting and showing me the sights. Wendi had been my right-hand woman before starting the tour, helping me to plan many of the hospital visits and my route through the states. Thank you again Wendi!

November 20, 2018

RUSH University Medical Center

Chicago, Illinois

Thank you to Shirley for an amazing morning! Upstairs (6th floor) was quite the scene. The nurses came out to dance, egg shake, and there were smiles and laughs for everyone. We took a group picture at the end.

I appreciate the time and efforts of the staff, day in and day out, in providing the best environment for your patients.

Happy holiday season! It's in the air!!

#rushmedicalcenter #holidaysarehere #musicismedicine

#13 INDIANA

SURPRISE HOME VISIT

===================

Before leaving, I am so thankful I was able to visit one of my childhood friends, Galen, and his family just outside of Chicago in Evanston, Illinois. Galen's grandfather was terminally ill and had invited me to stop into their home and play him some of his favorite songs.

Galen and his grandfather, Grandpa Bill.

November 21, 2018

Cedar Creek Assisted Living, Home visit, Gold Star Cafe

Lowell/Lafayette Indiana

Happy Thanksgiving!!

Given that this was going to be the first Thanksgiving I have ever been away from my family, I had 2 wishes... One, to play music for and help bring joy to those not fortunate enough to have family and/or afford the comforts of a traditional Thanksgiving meal. And two, if I wasn't able to enjoy dinner with my own family, I was hoping another would take me in. Well, both wishes came true!

Thank you to Tracy Prasco and her husband, having never met either of them, for housing me for two nights! She also escorted me to a home visit to meet Peyton (pictured on the next page with his sister and brother), whose humor and positive attitude will beat any sickness and hardship, guaranteed. "Peyton Shake" buddy! (We made up our own dance). TEAM PEYTON is strong! Tracy then brought me to visit the Cedar Creek Assisted Living facility where we all joined in playing music together, as well as visited individual rooms. We finished on Thanksgiving morning visiting Gold Star Cafe, where the owner fed people free Thanksgiving meals all day. She stopped the entire restaurant, introduced me, and let me play songs for the patrons as they enjoyed their meals. Such a blessing. Thank you Tracy. You're amazing!

#musicismedicinetour #happyturkeyday #wearealltogether

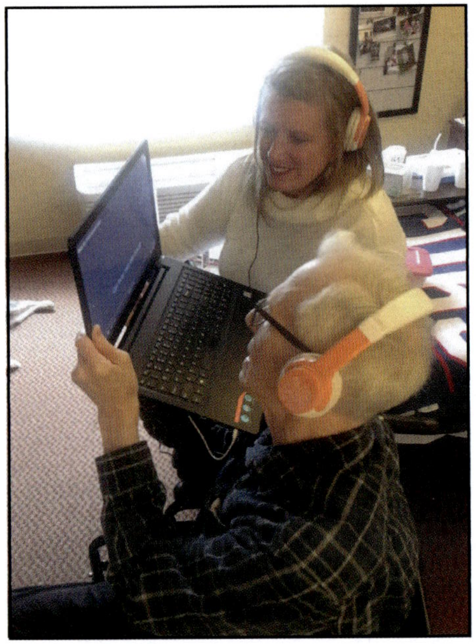

Tracy, singing with a resident at Cedar Creek Assisted Living.

(QR Code above) of our drum circle with the residents!

(QR Code above) of the home visit to meet Peyton and see his "floss dance" skills!

(Left), Peyton in green, with his brother, sister and I.

November 22, 2018

Lafayette, Indiana

Thanksgiving Dinner

Thank you to Abbey Smit for taking me in and inviting me to her grandma's house to meet and have dinner with her parents, brothers, cousins, and entire family for Thanksgiving! I couldn't have asked for a better way to spend the holiday on the road - food, music, love, and warmth! Happy Thanksgiving everyone.

#homeawayfromhome #longdistancefamily

#14 MICHIGAN

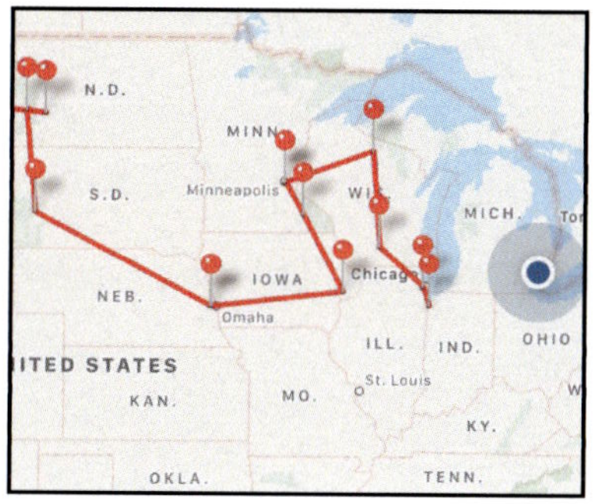

MOTOR CITY

============

I took the first day I arrived in Michigan to visit Detroit, the "Motor City." I enjoyed looking across the river into Canada and walking through Greek Town. I also visited the University of Michigan Campus in Ann Arbor.

MUSICAL SANTA!

===============

Thanksgiving was over now and I realized it was time for the holidays. Was there a way I could incorporate the Christmas spirit into my hospital visits? After a talk with a friend in San Diego and a visit to Walmart, I realized I could hand out gifts to the children and patients! These gifts however, would be egg shakers and beads out of my musical Santa sack! I would also dress in a Santa shirt, Christmas flannel, and musical holiday socks. Let the "musical holiday medicine" begin!

C.S. MOTT CHILDREN'S HOSPITAL

November 26, 2018

C.S. Mott Children's Hospital

Ann Arbor, Michigan

Ah, the holidays. I forget how much joy they can bring. I played Christmas songs and handed out 75 egg shakers today to children as they walked in and out of surgery. The simple joy of a little shake. My favorite is the sound the shakers make in each of the children's pockets as they run with them down the hallways. :)

Here's to the holidays, and the joy and reminder they bring for all of us to enjoy family and to be together. Thank you to University Of Michigan Mott Children's Hospital for welcoming me and letting me play for their patients and families! Greg Maxwell and Byron Myer - you gentlemen do great work. It's officially the Holiday Season!

#mottchildrens #musicismedicine #happyholidays

November 27, 2018

Walmart parking lot

Ann Arbor, Michigan

Thank you to Helen, a woman I met as I was standing on top of the hood of my Jambulance fixing a leak. It was dumping snow, and she kindly offered to book me a hotel room for the night. Her daughter was also a musician and Helen wanted to support the tour as best she could. Thank you Helen! It was much appreciated!

#thankyou #warminsideandout
#musicismedicinetour

Making some minor fixes to the Jambo before meeting Helen.

#15 OHIO

AHH, THE MID-WEST

=================

While in Ohio, I stayed with the Shepperd family. I had not met them before, but I would be joining them at an event at Akron Children's Hospital. During my stay, I was standing in the Shepperd's backyard. I asked Andy, the father of the family, "Where are your kids?"

"Not sure," he answered. "Probably at one of the neighbor's houses."

My favorite part, was that there were no fences separating the neighbors' yards from one another. "So your kids just roam from yard to yard, house to house?" I asked.

"Yep, pretty much." he answered with a smile.

It gave me just a small taste for mid-west neighborhoods, and I loved it.

December 1, 2018

Akron Children's Hospital

Akron, Ohio

Rarely do you meet someone as passionate, driven, and charismatic as Andrew Shepperd. Andy is the creator of Project Outrun, a non-profit organization whose mission is to put custom designed Nike I.D. shoes on kids battling pediatric cancer. I feel blessed to have been part such an impactful event, and to have met such an amazing group of people. Thank you Andy. Thank you Steph. And thank you to all the amazing volunteers that showed me what true team success can look like. Thank you also to Sara Kinnamon Fritsch for linking us together!

#projectoutrun #imnotsickbutmyshoesare #tooquicktobesick

Check out Project Outrun!
(QR Code - left)

#16 VERMONT

December 4, 2018

Rutland, Vermont

HAPPY HOLIDAYS everyone!! It's official - The Jambulance is ready to pull the sleigh of music and joy to hospitals across New England and the east coast!! Red nose, antlers and all. Here's to the joy and smiles of the holidays!

#jambulance #rudolph #tistheseason

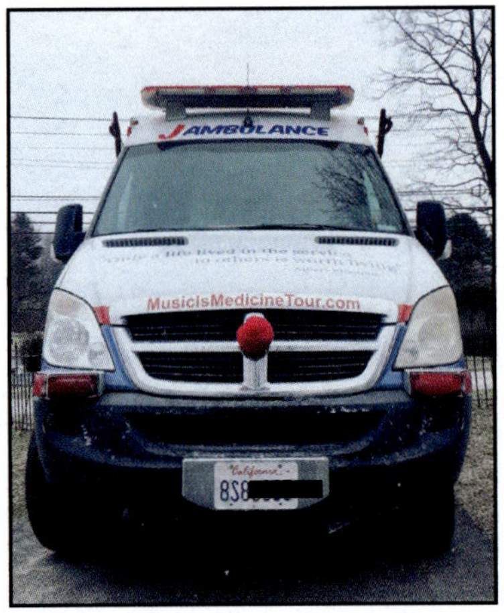

SKIING & MAPLE SYRUP

====================

When I arrived in Vermont, I knew I had to taste its famous maple syrup. After all, Vermont is the nation's leading producer! Vermont also has 20 alpine ski areas! Although I didn't ski, I was impressed with such a variety of mountains in such a small state.

December 5, 2018

The Pines at Rutland

Center for Nursing and Rehabilitation

Rutland, Vermont

It is not always easy playing music for the elderly. There is often very little reaction to noises or movement around them. It was challenging for me when I first started volunteering years ago not to take it personally, as I wondered if I was annoying them or if they even wanted me there at all! I have now learned, however, that they need music and enjoy interaction more than any other age group! Yesterday was a prime example of this. I'll never forget the end of playing "This Little Light of Mine." As if I was surrounded by 30 little angels having just woken up from their naps, singing softly to the chorus. I didn't want to stop playing as I teared up listening. Any coincidence that the song be about a light shining from within? I think not.

Thank you to Jessica Haney, who invited me to play here many months ago when the tour was first starting. This was the town she grew up in as well as where her mother works presently! So happy I got to meet her and all of the residents!

Here's to the eternal light within. Although never out, it is often our acknowledgment of it that keeps it ablaze.

#lightwithin #eternal #musicismedicine

#17 NEW HAMPSHIRE

LIVE FREE OR DIE!

================

What a beautiful drive. I'll never forget the transition from woodsy and mellow Vermont, into the beginning of the Revolutionary era and the colonial states - as New Hampshire's motto reads, "Live Free Or Die!"

Thank you to Hien and Haley for letting me stay at their house as well as showing me around the town of Dartmouth. I also got a tour of the Tuck School of Business, where Hien was a student. It was an eye opener for me, as I had never set foot on an Ivy League campus.

December 6, 2018

Dartmouth-Hitchcock Medical Center

Lebanon, New Hampshire

Thank you to Marianne Barthel for all the music and programs you bring to the patients and families at Dartmouth-Hitchcock Medical! So grateful I got to be a small part of the music yesterday.

Thank you also to Hien and Hailey for taking me in for 2 nights and showing me the beautiful town and college of Dartmouth University!

Happy Holidays!

#happyholidays #musicismedicinetour #ivyleague

#18 MAINE

December 9, 2018

Cape Elizabeth, Maine

From the Pacific to the Atlantic!! We did it! I've always wanted to stare out at the other side of this beautiful country. Thank you everyone for the support the entire way. Feels like we've been together this entire time.

#pacifictoatlantic #destinymanifest #50hospitals50states #musicismedicinetour

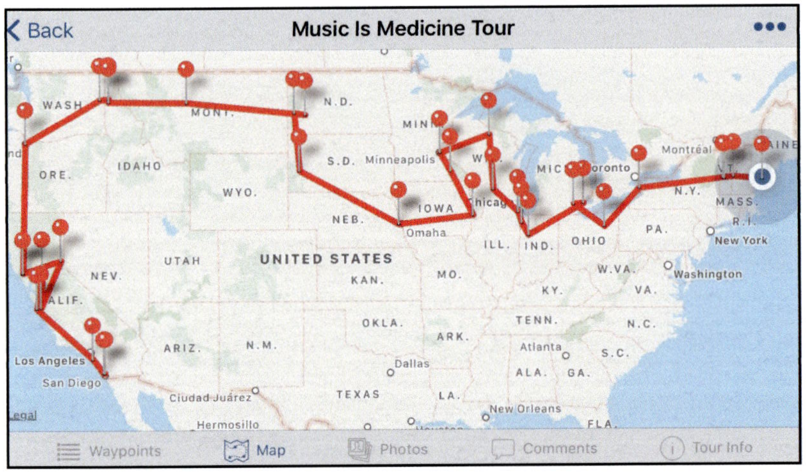

COAST TO COAST! Above, a map of my route including all hospital stops! From the Pacific coast of California to the Atlantic coast of Maine!

LOBSTER & LIGHTHOUSES

==========================

Two main things I knew about Maine was that they had great lobster and breathtaking lighthouses. I found both. Walking around the streets was a little bit like walking around San Francisco, only colder. The night I ordered lobster was amusing, as I little to no experience cracking and opening a lobster myself. The bartender at the restaurant where I ate, could tell. She ended up cracking and opening it for me ;)

Thank you to Nick Frank, a friend of mine who gifted me 2 nights in a hotel while in Maine. It was very cold and I was getting a little run down. I could sense my immune system was weakening, and the warm hotel nights were just what I needed.

December 10, 2018

Ronald McDonald House

Barbara Bush Children's Hospital

Portland, Maine

To have started this entire tour at the Ronald McDonald House in San Diego, and now be playing at another one on the completely other end of the country in Portland, Maine... well, it was meant to be. Thank you to Georgia Doucette, who reached out to me after hearing I was in town and fed me, gave me a full tour of the facility, and invited me to play for the children. The best part was singing Christmas songs in the kitchen with the children, where they were baking cookies for the holidays. We all danced around a make-believe Christmas tree in the middle. (I had placed my Christmas sack of egg shakers to act as such ;) Georgia then brought me over to the Barbara Bush Children's Hospital. It was an honor to play for the children there, especially after President Bush's recent passing.

If it interests you, I left a "QR code" below to learn more about the Ronald McDonald Houses and their history. It's an inspiring story involving an NFL football player and a corporate sponsor, collaborating to help fill a need.

It's also worth noting how amazing these houses are. It is beautiful how many thousands of families from all over the world they house and take care of while their children are being looked after at nearby hospitals, all free of charge! A mother and son I sang to today were from Rwanda, Africa!

Thank you Georgia, and thank you to all the Ronald McDonald Houses across America for doing all that you do for the families and children in need.

#ronaldmcdonaldhouse #barbarabushchildrenshospital

(QR Code right) - Ronald McDonald House history

THE "MAINE MOMENT"

=====================

Before leaving Maine, I pulled into a Whole Foods parking lot to rest up. I was excited to get some food at a location other than from Walmart! As I turned off the engine, I saw a man approaching me and walking straight toward the front of the Jambulance. He was tall, large in stature, bearded, and was wearing a baseball cap. He was approximately 2 rows of cars away and had both his hands up in the air as if he was angry about something. I could hear him yelling but couldn't make out the words. I wasn't sure at first if he was aiming his aggression at me, so I cracked the passenger window to listen more carefully. As he approached closer, there was no doubt he was coming toward me. I leaned over as to lead him to the passenger side rather than the driver's side window, and rolled it half-way down.

"Hi, can I help you with something?" I asked with a concerned look on my face.

"Yah, what's this whole 'Jambulance' thing about anyway?" he asked in a taunting manner as he put quotations with his fingers around the word "Jambulance."

His question was asked as though it was ridiculous that I would be driving such a vehicle, and that he seemed offended by me doing so. He had at least lowered his voice enough for us to have a somewhat normal conversation by now and had apparently been yelling his question numerous times as he had crossed the parking lot toward me.

"Hi," I said, but knew because of his temper that this was no time for small talk. "I'm driving across the country, playing music for people in hospitals and children with cancer."

As I finished my sentence, there was a silence. As his mouth opened to say what he previously wanted to say, he paused, as if time for him had stopped. He blinked once, mouth still open, and tilted his head to the side as an animal does when they're trying to understand. His gaze and his head started to lower toward the ground as both of his hands gripped the window frame of my passenger side door. I had never seen someone's body language change so quickly and dramatically in my life.

As if something had hit him like a ton of bricks, five seconds later he looked up at me with tears in his eyes and said, "I lost both my parents to cancer." He paused, looked down and back up again. "Both my mom, and my dad."

I closed my eyes and took a deep breath. Before I could say a word, he had turned around to get something out of his grocery cart. He turned back to me with a small brown box in his hands, held it out in front of himself and said, "I just got out of Whole Foods. I filled this box with my favorite salad and all my favorite things at the salad bar. I would be honored if you would take it. I don't have any cash to give you, but please take it as a token of thanks for what you're doing."

I nodded my head with a subtle smile and took the box. I placed it on the passenger seat and thanked him. I could tell he was embarrassed for his behavior earlier. I leaned over and reached out my hand.

"I'm sorry to hear about your parents. My name is Ryan."

We shook hands, and as he put his hands in prayer he backed away toward his cart. That was it. I rolled up the passenger window, took a deep breath, and sat in silence. My mouth and eyes slowly opened as I sat in shock at what had just transpired.

For the rest of the tour I would carry this experience with me. Realizing that wherever this "Jambulance" was to go, there was a chance to make a difference in another's life. An extreme difference, and yes, even in a grocery store parking lot.

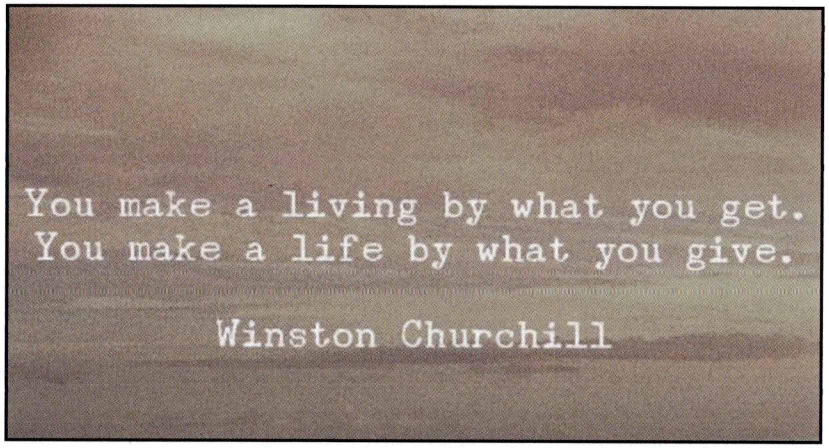

#19 MASSACHUSETTS

MY OWN DOCTOR VISIT

====================

I left Maine, and rolled south into Peabody, Massachusetts. By the way, if you ever visit Peabody make sure you pronounce it, 'PEA-buddie', with the emphasis on the first syllable. Those east-coasters are passionate about their accents, especially if it's regarding where they live!

As I previously had described in Maine, I was feeling a little run-down. I knew it was time to finally put my ego in check and go see a doctor. I had realized this tour was not about me and that my health had a direct impact on the people I was visiting in the hospitals. If I didn't take care of myself, the tour would not continue.

December 12, 2018

Care Well Urgent Care

Peabody, Massachusetts

What does a Music Is Medicine touring musician do, when he checks himself into a doctor for a common cold? He self-medicates! As I showed up to Urgent Care in Peabody, Massachusetts with a stuffy nose and sinus headache, I realized I wasn't the only one who wasn't feeling well. The waiting room had in it a family, a woman waiting for her husband, and the front desk attendant sitting quietly. After filling out my paperwork, I went to grab an egg shaker for the little boy who was with his mom and dad. 5 minutes later, I had my guitar, my Santa sack, and was singing Christmas songs to everyone waiting! Soon the nurses, doctors, and other staff members came out to witness a different kind of medicine being performed with their patients. Needless to say, the joy of singing and egg-shaking as a preliminary screening was an approved prescription by all.

Thank you to Ashley Queenan who answered the call and took my appointment, and especially for allowing us to sing and let music do its work!

Diagnosis? Music IS Medicine.

#musiceverywhere #bewell #musicismedicinetour

My band-mate & his family in the waiting room ;)

AMHERST, BOSTON, FREEDOM WALK

==================================

Thank you to Woody, Jamila, & Daniella Sherman for a relaxing break from the tour for a couple days in Amherst, Massachusetts! Thank you also to Angela for showing me around Boston and the Freedom Walk. What a beautiful city, and what an amazing way to learn more about the roots of American history!

December 15, 2018

Brigham & Women's Hospital

Boston, Massachusetts

So amazing to see so many hospitals located so closely and working together. Brigham & Women's, Boston Children's, Dana Farber Cancer Institute, and Beth Israel are all within a few blocks of each other in Downtown Boston. One of the most meaningful parts of the tour thus far, was to visit Brigham & Women's Hospital.

A few years ago, one of my close friends from college passed away at Brigham & Women's Hospital. When I first began this journey, his wife asked if I could possibly visit and play music here. She spoke of how wonderful and supportive the staff was, and that it would mean the world to her if I could visit those who took care of him. Needless to say, before I knew it, I was in the ICU where my friend was cared for until he passed. I played music for the patients there hoping to provide love and an uplifting sound in their time of need.

Thank you to LB Gadsby, for her courage and willingness to not only respect and heal her past, but to openly step forward and dedicate the same love into the future. As his presence and love was felt strong both en route to Brigham Women's and while there, Brian Lowen lives on forever.

#musicismedicine #musicismedicinetour #livesonforever

#20 RHODE ISLAND

CLIFF WALK

==========

Walking along the coastal Cliff Walk in Newport was one of my favorite walks of the tour. It was beautiful to see all of the old colonial houses and buildings, as well as to be looking out over a completely opposite coast and the Atlantic Ocean.

December 17, 2018

The Hot Club/Hasbro Children's Hospital

Providence, Rhode Island

Sometimes you hear of something you just know you have to be a part of. This, I knew, was one of them.

Over a year ago after playing music at a restaurant in La Jolla, California, a woman at one of the tables had told me that I needed to include Providence, Rhode Island, as one of my stops on the tour. She said to visit a bar called, "The Hot Club." She had explained to me that the entire restaurant stops, hands out flashlights to all the patrons, and flashes them on and off to say goodnight to the children of the neighboring hospital.

The video (below) says it all, and I feel blessed to have been a part of such an amazing tradition. I not only got to "say goodnight" to the children of Hasbro, but I got to sing to these same children the next day.

Thank you to The Hot Club, to Hasbro Children's Hospital, and to all the community members of Providence that make this simple yet impactful tradition, possible.

#goodnightlights #musicismedicine #everylittlebithelps

I can't help but think of the tour's mantra, "See the light, Be the light" every time I watch the video to the right. Enjoy :)

#21 CONNECTICUT

December 19, 2018

Essex Meadows Senior Living

Essex, Connecticut

One of the best experiences and friendships one could ask for on the tour thus far.

After playing music at Shriners Children's Hospital in Twin Cities, Minneapolis in November, Nancy Easter, a pediatric care worker there, had told me about her mother who lived in a senior living facility in Essex, Connecticut. She had asked me if it would be possible to make a stop on the tour to visit her mom. Well, 21 states in and a month and a half later, I called and told her I was in Connecticut and would love to! I not only loved seeing the beautiful, quaint little Connecticut river-town of Essex, but left with a new friend. And, my first mink coat!

Nancy, your mother is the most spry, humorous, genuine 91-year-old woman I have ever met. My favorite line of the day with her... "Margie," I said, "It was a joy playing music for your fellow residents. I've got about an hour left. What is it you'd like to do?"

I assumed we'd probably sit down not far from the room I played in and chat over a cup of tea or coffee. Instead she responded with, "Well first off, I insist you take this old mink coat of mine. I'm sure you could use more warm clothes on the road and I want to contribute to the cause! I also figured," she continued, "we'd take a little spin in your Jambulance and check out the town of Essex!"

Margie, you inspire me and everyone who crosses your path. May we all possess even half the light you have inside!

#musicismedicine #newfriends #kidatheart

Marjorie, awaiting her ride in the Jambulance!

The "mink coat"

#22 NEW YORK

NIAGARA FALLS

===================

I had been to New York and had heard of Niagara Falls growing up, but had never actually seen the falls myself. At 75,000 gal/second, you could hear the surging yet calming roar of the water as it crashed below. Once again, I was staring over at the Canadian border. Thank you to Jessica Glose for the hospitality, time with your beautiful family, and taking me to see one of the most beautiful waterfalls in the world!

FAMILY SURPRISE!!

====================

One of the highlights of being in New York City was being able to see my brother, his wife Kelsey, and my one year-old niece! They flew in from Lake Tahoe just in time so we could see each other and explore the city. It was my niece's first time to New York so the big city was an eye opener!

December 21, 2018

Brooks Brothers

Madison Ave, New York City

What better way to end the first half of the tour, than to receive a grant in the amount of $1,000 from Brooks Brothers, New York! Thank you to Monica Fineis for her hard work in making this happen, and her recognition of both the Music Is Medicine Tour and the Alive Inside Foundation as worthy recipients!

10 years ago, I was told by one of my closest friends that I needed to watch a documentary called, "Alive Inside." The movie takes you into the homes and facilities of elderly and seniors with dementia, where music and song are used as a way for them to once again capture their memories and events of the past. What better organization than Alive Inside for me to partner with?! Well, thank you to Michael Rossato-Bennett, Tai Campbell, and the Alive Inside Foundation for saying yes to teaming up with me when this tour was first in it's incubation stage 7-8 months ago. I have been able to use their 501c3 non-profit status as a means for those wanting to use donations as write-offs. Without this ability, as well as Michael's continued mentorship and example, this tour would not be where it is today. For those of you who have NOT watched the "Alive Inside" documentary, please do, and get ready to be both shocked and inspired. (QR Code website to right)

Happy Holidays everyone, and Merry Christmas. Thank you all for being such an amazing support.

#aliveinside #brooksbrothersnewyork #merrychristmas

Michael (writer & director of *Alive Inside*) and I, receiving the grant check.

December 22, 2018

BROOKLYN HOSPITAL

Brooklyn, New York

Lastly, I was able to play music for patients entering Brooklyn Hospital and hand out egg shakers to children and families. It was so refreshing to see the smiles come across their face as they received a gift and a song during an otherwise somber or uneasy evening.

Thank you to Josh Allen for joining me and recording some amazing footage of a full day in New York City and life on the road!

#eggshakersbringsmiles

#brooklynhospital @joshallenimages

December 23 - January 4, 2019

BACK HOME FOR CHRISTMAS

Lake Tahoe, California

For those of you that didn't know, I left the Jambulance at a friend's house outside of Philadelphia for the last 2 weeks. I flew home to Lake Tahoe, California to see Santa Claus and spend time with my family and childhood friends. What a joy it was being home for the holidays. I feel so lucky to have a place to come home to, especially after being on the road for nearly 4 months! How fun to see my niece growing and changing every day, and to relax... truly relax. I had no idea how much different a nap was on the road, than when you're at home with a fire lit and nowhere you need to be!

Mom, Pops, Bro, Kels, Desa.. I love and appreciate time with you guys so much. Thank you for always being such a home for me.

#homeforholidays #family #merrychristmas

AN "AH-HAH!" TURNING POINT IN THE TOUR

==

While home for the Christmas holiday, I had gone to the gym to workout a few days with my dad. During one of my workouts, I had realized that being cooped up in the Jambulance day in and day out had taken a toll not only on my body, but on my mental happiness. Would it be possible to workout somehow while on the road? Could I find a gym in every state that wouldn't take me too far off my hospital route? Wait a second, what if I were able to get a membership with a 24-Hour Fitness type gym? They claim to have gyms across the entire country! Imagine taking showers, shaving, and working out every morning! After my own research, I found that Planet Fitness was the best fit for me. It was affordable, offered a welcoming environment, and it was open 24 hours! There were over 1,800 locations in the US, which was far more than any of the other major nation-wide gyms.

As I got back from Christmas and back to the Jambulance, I started my membership in Pennsylvania. This would soon become the biggest game changer for the second half of the tour. Besides being able to workout and shower, it also provided the majority of my overnight sleeping arrangements for the remaining 28 states! All in all, I worked out (and slept in the parking lot) at 22 different Planet Fitness locations!

Thank you Planet Fitness. You guys are a huge reason I survived the winter and was able to enjoy the journey as much as I did!

#23 PENNSYLVANIA

BACK ON THE ROAD

===================

I loved being home for the holidays, but was also excited to get back and start the tour again. I had missed meeting new people, visiting new hospitals, and playing music for those in need.

Thank you to the Behl family for showing me Philly and what the city stands for. Blue collar, loyal (sometimes with a chip on their shoulder), never-say-die mentality. It's no coincidence Rocky was filmed here.

January 9, 2019

Hospital of The University of Pennsylvania

Philadelphia, Pennsylvania

Thank you to David Cribb and the Hospital of The University of Pennsylvania, for allowing me to visit all 4 floors and the individual rooms of your hospital and cancer treatment centers! I showed up at 10 am, and left at 3 pm! Having never spent this long at a particular hospital before, I was welcomed in and blessed to meet and share in so many different conversations, songs, tears, and laughter. As I've said before, there is nothing I'd rather be doing, than be right back on this tour doing exactly this. Thank you Philly.

(QR code bottom right - a video of a patient who epitomizes the Philly spirit!)

#onlyinphilly #musicismedicine

#24 NEW JERSEY

ATLANTIC CITY

================

As I arrived in New Jersey I knew that I wanted to visit Atlantic City and the Jersey Shore. Because of the time of year, the shoreline and beaches were desolate. It was nice to walk the beach. Atlantic City was much like Las Vegas, only smaller. The highlight was heading into one of the large casino hotels to watch the NFL Draft! It makes you appreciate the little conveniences like TV when you go without it for over 4 months.

CHELSEA SENIOR LIVING®

January 14, 2019

Chelsea Senior Living

Helmetta, New Jersey

Chris Slavicek, ya beat me to it. I wanted to post about how thankful I am for you and the opportunity of being connected with you. One of the most passionate and committed public servants I have ever met. Chris, Mayor of Helmetta, New Jersey, also runs and maintains 18 different Senior Care facilities. I was blessed to play and visit 3 of them with him. We were followed by CBS News most of the day - the happiness and opportunities he brings to the residents here deserve to be recognized.

It was meant to be that we met, Chris, as I know you know

this. I want to thank you again for what you do, who you are, and what you stand for. ANY town would be blessed to have you as their mayor.

Thank you to Fran Pannella, who was affiliated with Alive Inside and gave my information to Chris and connected us in the first place. Without her, this part of the tour would have never happened!

#chelseaseniorliving #musicismedicine #aliveinside

Mayor Slavicek & Fran after our musical set!

#25 DELAWARE

FIRST STATE IN THE UNION!

========================

Here's to Delaware being the first state in the Union, and the nation's second smallest state! It was nice to drive south along the coast and the Delaware River. The river starts in New York and runs south 419 miles, eventually emptying into the Delaware Bay and Atlantic Ocean.

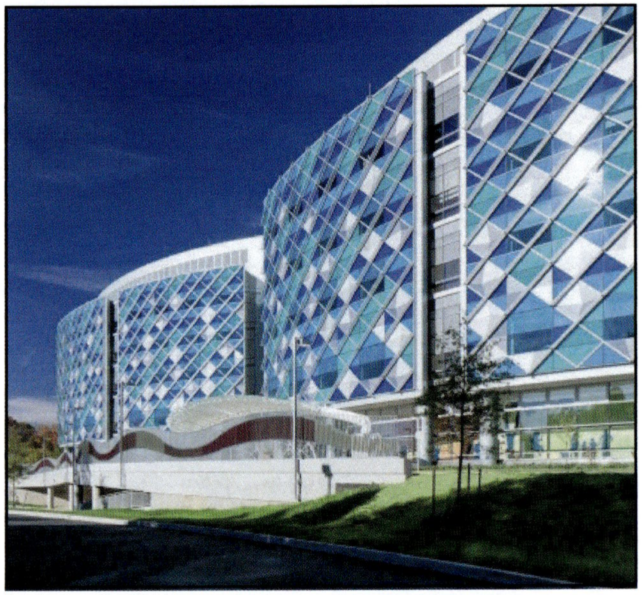

January 16, 2019

Kent General, Milford Memorial

A.I. DuPont Nemours Children's Hospital

Dover, Delaware

Thank you to Jane Hewett, Carrie Hart, and her staff for taking me in and bringing me to 3 different locations to play music for their residents, staff, and patients. I'll never forget singing with one of the patients who was once a choir teacher. Rarely did I ever get to sing duets in the visits I had made! Thank you Jane for being such an enthusiastic host, driving me to each location, and taking the time to teach me about Delaware. Jane was so enthusiastic that she called A.I. DuPont Children's Hospital in northern Delaware and booked me the day after I visited her! Rarely had I seen a children's hospital so bright and colorful for kids. There was also an amazing sound system for visiting musicians to use!

#musicismedicine #firststateinamerica #musicismedicinetour

Jane, outside the hospital placing the guitar on Delaware!

#26 MARYLAND / WASHINGTON D.C.

FORT MCHENRY & ANNAPOLIS

==============================

One of the highlights of traveling into Baltimore, was learning about Fort McHenry. I learned about how it was such a pivotal win in the War of 1812 against the British, as well as the place where the Star Spangled Banner was written! This was a fun fact for me, as I had always assumed it was written during the Revolutionary War.

Annapolis was amazing. What a clean, beautiful, historic town. I was able to meet for lunch with the mother and sister of a friend of mine who lived nearby and showed me the sites. I also enjoyed taking a tour of the campus of the United States Naval Academy.

WASHINGTON D.C.

==================

The last time I visited Washington D.C. was in 6th grade. Getting to take in all of the sights now as an adult, was special. The Arlington Cemetery, JFK's eternal flame, and standing in front of the White House were the highlights of my visit.

JOHNS HOPKINS MEDICAL

==========================

What a memorable day, visiting Johns Hopkins Hospital and meeting with Dr. Alex Pantelyat. Dr. Pantelyat, once a professional musician himself, is now the Co-Director of the Johns Hopkins Center for Music and Medicine. He now uses both of his passions to help heal his patients. We had been in touch since I started the tour, and it was such an honor to meet him in person and talk about the work he has done in the field of using music as medicine.

Photo: Johns Hopkins Medicine

January 18, 2019

The Johns Hopkins Hospital

Baltimore, Maryland

====================

What an amazing experience to be the bridge between 2 men I look up to both as mentors and leaders in the world of music and medicine.

(Above/right) is a FaceTime screen shot of Dr. Alex Pantelyat, the Co-Director of the Johns Hopkins "Center for Music and Medicine", and Michael Rossato Bennett, writer and director of the "Alive Inside" documentary film (mentioned earlier in Chapter 22, New York). They had never met before, but knew of each other, and each had respect for the work the other had done.

Before the tour, I had reached out to both of them. 6 months later, here each of us were, talking and brainstorming and sharing our passions together in the world of music being used as medicine!

It was an honor gentlemen to have met you both and to have witnessed a conversation that I know will bear fruit into the future!

#johnshopkinshospital #aliveinside #musicandthebrain

Please watch the "Healing Power of Music" video (left), and the amazing work Dr. Pantelyat and his staff do at The John's Hopkins Center for Music & Medicine!

#27 VIRGINIA

WASHINGTON & JEFFERSON

===========================

Virginia just reeked of history. You could sense the Civil War and it's battles, the heroes, and the presidents. While driving, I felt like I could literally see and hear the gunshots through the aspen trees as soldiers ran through hiding and ducking behind them. I had seen so many reenactments and movies about the Civil War that I felt like I were right there with them!

I felt so lucky to learn about and visit the houses of men like George Washington and Thomas Jefferson. General Washington fought in and led armies into 3 battles! Thomas Jefferson was Minister to France, Governor of Virginia, author of the Declaration of Independence, Secretary of State, Vice President and President of United States - all before the age of 33!

Birmingham Green

January 24, 2019

Birmingham Green Health Care

Manassas, Virginia

How awesome it was to call a past middle school student of mine who is now a nurse. She has graduated from college, has started a career she loves, and is looking to further her education even more as a nurse practitioner! I surprised her and booked a time to come and play for her patients & residents at the nursing home where she now works!

Thank you Amor, for spending the time to check out Virginia with me and welcome me in to come and play music for your residents and patients. 10 years later, here we are!

#proudteacher #birminghamgreen #musicismedicinetour

#28 WEST VIRGINIA

BIG HEART

============

"Almost Heaven, West Virginia, cool ridge mountains, Shenandoah River. Life is old there, older than the trees, younger than the mountains, growin' like a breeze."

- John Denver, Take Me Home Country Roads

To the people of West Virginia and the Appalachian Mountains, thank you for the impact you had on me, and the tour on you. Some of my favorite moments were when I would go to eat somewhere. By the time my meal was over, I would leave with new friends. I respect the simple and content way of life people seem to live here. You can hear it in the way they speak and interact with one another. I was in the mountains, but felt like I was in the country. What a beautiful combination.

Pictured (far left) are of a group of waitresses at one of the local restaurants who couldn't wait to come out and see the Jambulance! (Immediate left) is Brandon, who changed my oil in Dunbar, West Virginia. We are still in touch today.

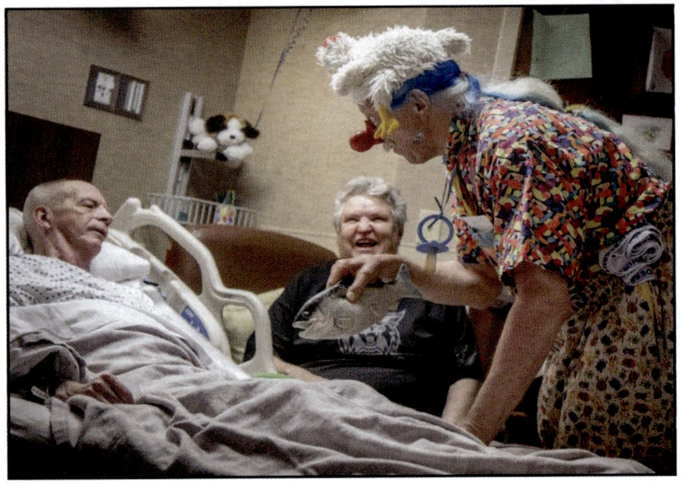

January 27, 2019

Gesundheit Institute

Hillsboro, West Virginia

~DEDICATED TO BAILEY MCDONALD~ (QR Code above)

What better place to dedicate a visit to Bailey McDonald, than at the home of a man whose goal in life is to spread joy, laughter, and love to those who need it most!

20 years ago, I watched a movie well-known to most of you called, Patch Adams. It is a true story about a medical student whose passion became more about bringing humor and establishing rapport with patients, than to use traditional medicinal techniques. His goal? To open a FREE HEALTH CLINIC available to any and all people needing medical attention, with the emphasis on the overall "patient" rather than their sickness. After watching the movie, I was in tears and feeling more inspired than I had ever felt before. Not only did it become my favorite movie, but Patch Adams quickly became a mentor and a hero to me.

Well, here I sit at the Gesundheit Institute in Hillsboro, West Virginia. It is home to Patch and his non-traditional, unorthodox, humorous, outlandish, and perfectly planned medicinal techniques. He still runs workshops and retreats here today. The Institute spans out over 321 acres and has hiking, a pond for swimming, wood shop, painting, clowning, and just about anything else you could imagine that would bring a smile to your face!

Thank you Patch, for inspiring me for the last 20 years. You've shown me, by example, that I too can make a difference in the lives of others by connecting and accepting them exactly where they are, and by using my own "unorthodox", "non-traditional" ways of bringing healing to others.

Thank you also to Adam Craten who care-takes the property. Adam took an hour and a half out of his morning, walked me into every room, every floor, took me around the entire property and taught me everything he knew about Patch and the history of the Gesundheit Institute.

I'll be back here again. I will also meet Patch Adams. And I won't be surprised in the slightest if I create and open a property much like here at the Gesundheit Institute in Hillsboro, West Virginia. Bailey, you'll be here waiting. I feel you already.

#dedication #bailey #patchadams #humorismedicine

#29 KENTUCKY

POLAR VORTEX!!

==================

I had just arrived to Kentucky when the "polar vortex" hit. There were record lows in the country for weather and I was very thankful I wasn't any farther north. In Louisville (dark blue on map below), it was below 5 degrees outside and this was without question one of those times I needed to find a hotel and get inside. As you can see below, other parts of the country just north of me had temperatures as low as negative 33 degrees! The news told people not to leave the house, go to the store, or go outside at all! Many workplaces were closed as well as schools. I took a time-out, got a hotel for 2 nights, and played it safe.

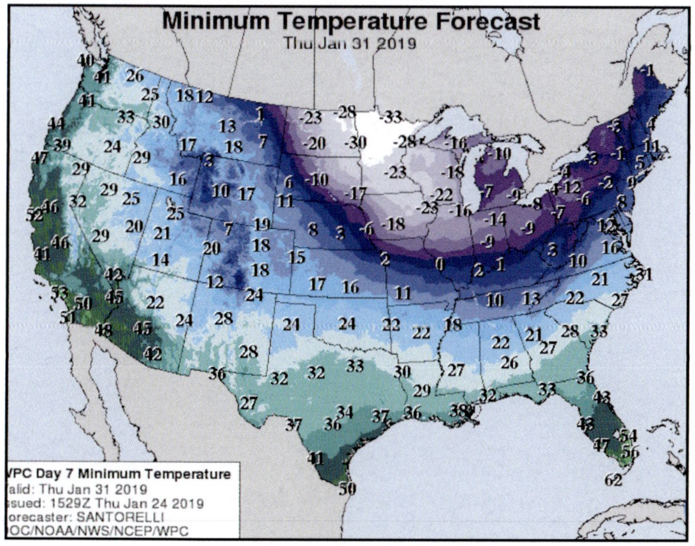

February 1, 2019

University of Kentucky Health Care

Lexington, Kentucky

Thank you Kentucky. Much like West Virginia, the people here seem to be simple, easy going, and honest. The group of music therapists (pictured above) joined me during the entire performance, singing and playing the instruments I handed them. This was definitely the most participation I've had from staff in any hospital yet! Quite a treat to be able to harmonize and have consistent rhythm with the egg shakers for every song!

Thank you to Jason Akhtarekhavari and Cheryl Benz, for welcoming me into their hospital and letting me play for their patients and staff. The Integrative Medicine and Music Therapy department was very impressive. I hope you will all continue to be a model for music therapy in hospitals, as well as integrative medicines of all kinds across the nation!

#ukhealthcare #musictherapy #musicismedicinetour

#30 NORTH CAROLINA

A DURHAM SUPER BOWL

======================

Ahh, warmer weather. When I arrived, it was 64 degrees! My middle name is Durham, so since I was a child I always wondered what the town of Durham looked like and where it was located. What an awesome town. I also felt so blessed to be able to visit Pj, Misty, and their son Maddox. As you may remember, I dedicated my visit in West Virginia to their daughter, Bailey. Pj grew up in Boston, so it was perfect to watch the Patriots win (yet another) Super Bowl with him.

February 6, 2019

Duke Raleigh Hospital

Raleigh, North Carolina

What an amazing day today. I've noticed little by little along this tour, how important and refreshing it seems for nurses and other staff members in the hospital to enjoy music during my visits as well. Although most of this tour is focused on playing music for patients and residents, every once in a while you've got to feed musical medicine to the nurses and staff too! After all, if you give THEM energy - they give it right back to the ones they care for!

Thank you to Zachary Baker and his team, who took me in and brought me to every single floor of the hospital. Yes I sang for patients, but by the time I left each floor, I had managed to acquire yet another new set of friends and band members!

Here's to the doctors, nurses, and staff members in all hospitals, who day in and day out give of themselves to others in need! And here's to stopping and refueling with a little dancin' and singin' so that you can give even more!

#becausenursesneedmusictoo #dukeraleighhospital

#31 SOUTH CAROLINA

FIRST SHOTS FIRED

======================

I had no idea that South Carolina was the first state to secede from the Union prior to the Civil War. I arrived there thinking I wasn't going to be in the "south" until states like Georgia, Alabama, and Mississippi. The museums here were amazing. I was actually asked to leave one of them due to me unknowingly staying 20 minutes past closing time! I was so interested in learning about the Civil War and where it started - right here at Fort Sumter.

Charleston, South Carolina, was an adorable town straight out of a magazine. I felt like I was stuck right in the middle of the Colonial times. The canons were still placed in their original spots, the houses were absolutely gorgeous, and the entire town was nestled right up along the coast.

FUN FACT: The tree on the state flag (upper left) is the palmetto tree, giving honor to its protection during the Revolutionary War. Fort Sullivan's walls were fortified with palmetto logs. Rather than shattering like most other types of wood, they absorbed the force from the cannonballs during the War of 1812. Hence, honoring the palmetto tree on the state flag.

February 11, 2019

Shriners Hospital for Children

Greenville, South Carolina

Again, I was impressed. The first Shriners Hospital I visited was in Spokane, Washington. The second one I stopped at was in Twin Cities, Minnesota. And now, I had the privilege to play for the children of Greenville, South Carolina. Each of these hospitals were equally impressive. Thank you to Trana Pritta, Shriners' volunteer coordinator, for facilitating the entire day. A special thank you also to Nancy Miller Easter, a social worker at Shriners Hospital for Children in Twin Cities, Minnesota, who reached out and connected the story of the tour with yet another Shriners Hospital!

#shrinerschildrenshospital #musicismedicine #musicismedicinetour

South Carolina gets their guitar!

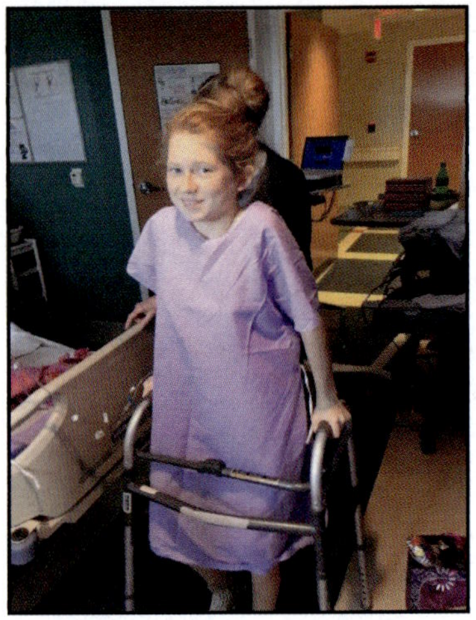

Dominique, 12 years old, after one of her many surgeries.

"NEVER STOP FIGHTING"

======================

Hi, my name is Dominique Rapien. I am 18 years old and live in Easley, South Carolina. I have been a patient at Shriners Hospital for Children in Greenville, South Carolina for 17 years. I met Ryan during the Music Is Medicine Tour when he came and played music for us in February of 2019. I am writing this letter to help any child or young adult who is reading this book, to know that they are not alone in any challenges they might face in their lives. By reading a bit about my story, I would hope that it could help you get through challenges in your own life. If I can get through rough times, I know and believe that you can too!

I was born on January 21, 2002, in Greenville, South Carolina. Before I could walk, the doctors noticed something wrong with my feet and Achilles tendon. When I was 7 the doctors found out that I had "CMT", also known as "Charcot-Marie-Tooth". CMT is a neurological disorder and a form of peripheral neuropathy, meaning it affects the nerves and muscles in the arms, legs, hands, and feet. It caused me to not be able to walk, I couldn't feel the bottom part of my legs, and it was difficult to sleep at night. I had to wear a brace until I was age 6 or 7. I also wasn't able to dance or play sports when I was little because of the CMT. Lastly, I was made fun of a lot in school because I could hardly walk up and down stairs because of my casts. No matter how much I wanted to do things like a normal kid, I couldn't. Let's just say growing up wasn't easy.

My first piece of advice for anyone going through an unfortunate event, circumstance, or disease in their life, is to be thankful for the support around them. Without my mom and dad, I never would have been able to make it. With their support, I really started to believe that I could do anything I put my mind to! By age 8, I was racing go-karts. I also made it onto both the baseball and basketball teams. I joined middle school band and learned to play the clarinet. In 7th grade I joined the school marching band, and taught myself to play trumpet, baritone, and saxophone. By 11th grade I started playing saxophone and percussion in the school band! I was invited to be in the Governor's School for Mathematics and Science, a scholastic college prep program, from 9th to 10th grade. And lastly, I was just accepted last month to the College of Charleston for college! I will be starting my freshman year in September!

My plan moving forward is to work with children who are in similar situations as me and become a pediatric surgeon. I know how it feels to be in an unfortunate situation, and I want to help others as it might even be more difficult for them. I want to show them that nothing is impossible. Helping them will also make me want to keep going! If you are going through rough times in your life or have a disability, or a sickness or cancer of your own, just know that you are able to get through it! If you ARE one of these people or children, this letter is for you. Keep fighting. Never give up. Believe in something greater and more fun than your disability and sickness (like a sport or music or a hero of yours) and focus on that. We all have things happen to us in life - it's what we do with it that counts!

#32 GEORGIA

LAND OF PEACHES

==================

Savannah, Georgia, was one of my favorite towns that I drove through. There was a courtyard in the middle of town where families and children were playing, a variety of live music on several street corners, and it still somehow kept a quaint feel to it. On the way out of town I stopped at "Peach World," bought a jar of peaches and finished the entire jar within the first hour of driving!

"Life's most persistent and urgent question: What are you doing for others?" - Dr. Martin Luther King, Jr.

MARTIN LUTHER KING JR.

=======================

Atlanta, Georgia. What an amazing opportunity to visit the Martin Luther King Jr. National Historical Park, the house he grew up in, and the church his family attended while in his adolescent years. I spent all day walking down Auburn Avenue, trying to imagine how different it must have felt in the 50's and 60's.

February 13, 2019

Annandale Village

Suwanee, Georgia

How special it was to visit someone on my sister-in-law's side of the family.

Founded in 1969, Annandale Village is an award-winning non-profit organization dedicated solely to providing progressive life assistance to adults with developmental disabilities and acquired brain injuries. Tucked away on a beautiful 55-acre campus, Annandale Village is a special place where men and women with intellectual and developmental disabilities lead lives that reflect quality, independence, self-worth, and achievement with the utmost care and compassion.

I want to thank Julie Ferguson for inviting me to play music for the "villagers," which is what they all proudly call themselves. It was a day I will never forget. I have visited many hospitals and nursing homes on this trip, but this was the first of its kind. It makes me so happy to know there are places like this - that include men and women of all abilities who all feel welcome, valued, and in a place they call HOME. Thank you so much Annandale Village. You made me feel like a villager myself today. Happy Valentine's Day everyone!

#musicismedicinetour #annandalevillage #villagers

My cousin-in-law Jackie. We are holding a framed picture of Jackie's sister, Lynn, who asked me to come and pay Jackie a surprise visit! (Jackie's showing off her new Music Is Medicine guitar picks :)

#33 FLORIDA

DISNEY WORLD!!

================

Can't go to Florida and not go to Walt Disney World! Thank you to Judy and Bruce Wilson who were both teachers of mine growing up. Judy was once an employee at Disney World so I couldn't have asked for a better tour guide! What an amazing place. I was impressed with how well Disney featured different cultures and places from all over the world. The happiest place on earth definitely lived up to it's motto!

EVERGLADES NATIONAL PARK

===========================

What a unique landscape Florida has. From the beautiful everglades and humid swamplands, to the colorful coast of Miami, this state was unlike any other. It was incredible to me how nonchalant locals were about alligators. Within the first 5 minutes of walking into Everglades National Park, I had one swim underneath the wooden bridge I was walking over. As I froze and slowly walked backward off the bridge, everyone else smiled as if they thought the alligator was cute!

February 21, 2019

Home Visits

Jacksonville, Florida

What a start to the week. Playing songs and sharing the tour's story with a local family, interviewing a mother whose daughter at 3 years old has been in for multiple heart surgeries, and visiting the beautiful ranch of a man who had just found out he had cancer.

Thank you to Joanna Jones for hosting and putting such amazing experiences such as these together for us. Thank you also to Ian Bull, once again, for capturing all of it! I appreciate you both very much.

#thankful #family #musicismedicine

February 24, 2019

UF Health Shands Cancer Hospital

Gainesville, Florida

What a program! Shands Hospital not only has an impressive Arts & Music Program, they also pay their musicians and artists! This is the first of its kind I have encountered on the tour.

Thank you to Kris Sullivan, Michael Claytor, and the rest of the staff for letting me and my new wing-man, Ian Bull, come and be a part of an already amazing program. Thank you also to Brett Missick. Without his recommendation I would have never known to come here!

#musicismedicinetour #shandshospital #seethelight

February 25, 2019

Coastal Church

Daytona Beach, Florida

What an honor. The first time I have ever spoken to a church and I couldn't have asked for a better experience. Wesley Stewart, (Owner and CEO of Urban Surf 4 Kids), had asked me to come and speak to his congregation about being of service to others. I told him that I would be honored and that this topic would be perfectly aligned to the Music Is Medicine Tour.

Best part however, was coming out of the church to the majority of the congregation's children gathered around the Jambulance!! So awesome to tell them about the tour, answer any questions, and take pictures. Such an inspiration for all!

Thank you Wes. And thank you for the surf afterwards!!

#servicetoothers #musicismedicine

#musicismedicinetour

February 27, 2019

Home Visit

Miami, Florida

So amazing to be a part of something larger than myself. This tour has given me the chance to lose myself IN it, and TO it. Driving 7 hours to visit and play music for a woman I have never met in her home, is the result. We played music, talked about each of our experiences with diagnosis, and shared what we'd learned and are learning through the process. Best part, is that she is an amazing professional opera singer!! How fitting.

Angela, I admire you for so many reasons - your strength, love, and larger than life personality was a joy to be around. You are a bright light indeed. You inspire me to keep doing what I'm doing and to become even more of who I am. Thank you for welcoming me into your home. And thank you for being the light that you are! A big hug and thank you to Jill Meadows, who asked me over 2 months ago if this visit was possible. Thank you for making this connection and visit happen!! Love you Jilly.

#we'reallinthistogether #servicetoothers

#musicismedicine

#34 ALABAMA

SELMA BRIDGE

=================

Florida to Alabama - only one state away from each other and almost completely different worlds. As I walked over the Selma Bridge, it was like walking through a history book. I had seen the bridge portrayed both in movies and museums but to see it in person was an entirely different experience. I admire, more than words can explain, the courage of those that walked this bridge in a fight for freedom. May this same courage continue to help open the eyes and ears of future generations to come.

March 2, 2019

USA Children & Women's Hospital

Mobile, Alabama

Thank you to USA Children & Women's for having me! The best part was meeting and speaking with a new father outside. He too was a musician and thanked me for my music. His baby boy was born at 23 weeks, and he shared with me how his life had been put into perspective. I shared with him how my life had changed dramatically as well and after hearing the story of the tour, said he planned to go home and speak with his band about doing something similar.

You never know whose life can be affected positively by what you're doing. Here's to being our best wherever we go!

#musicismedicine #musicismedicinetour #rippleeffect

#35 LOUISIANA

MARDI GRAS

=================

I hadn't planned on it originally, but I came through Louisiana toward the beginning of March. I had never been to New Orleans, and "Fat Tuesday" and the festivities of Mardi Gras started on March 5th! The parades were non-stop, day and night. The people, the music, the food - wow. What a treat it was for me to take a time-out, park the Jambulance, and witness some of the best music and spirited festivities in the world!

March 6, 2019

Our Lady of the Lake Regional Medical Center

Baton Rouge, Louisiana

Sometimes the most rewarding part of the tour is not the people I play for, but the playing of the music itself. Same as when a painter loses himself/herself in the act of painting. Time is not a factor anymore and hours could go by before you know or care. It's the art and the music itself that brings peace to the one playing it.

This was my experience today while playing music for those at Our Lady Of The Lake Hospital in Baton Rouge, Louisiana. And for this, I am grateful.

#musicismedicine #loseyourself #musicismedicinetour

#36 MISSISSIPPI

TORNADO WATCH

====================

At least once a week during the tour, I would have people (my mom being the first of course :) inform me of any weather concerns coming my way. This one, however, was a first. Apparently there was a tornado headed east through Arkansas, Mississippi, Tennessee, and Alabama - exactly where my route was taking me! So, seeing that I had no experience being in this type of weather condition, as well as the fact that I was driving a 13-foot tall van with a metal rack on the top, I decided to stay put. I had just crossed over the southern border into a town called Magnolia, Mississippi. I ended up staying at a local gas station for 2 nights and 3 days, watching the weather and making friends with anyone who stopped by to get gas!

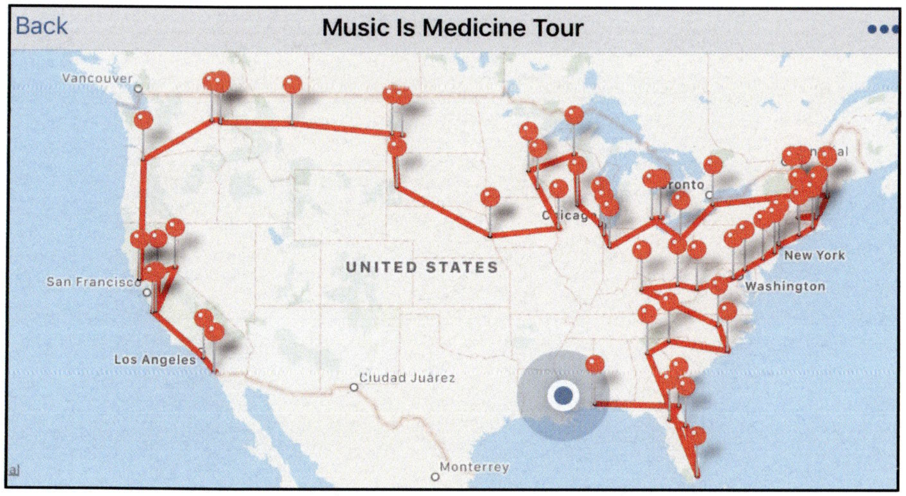

CONNECTION TO HOSPITAL

=========================

As fate would have it, one of the best connections I could have asked for while waiting for the tornado to pass, was meeting a family and their 3 daughters that had stopped in to get gas. The father, being inspired by the tour, called his wife and shared my story with her. It turns out she worked at a children's hospital 2 hours north in Jackson. After speaking with her, I was able to book a visit at the "Children's of Mississippi" hospital to play for the children there, (once the tornado had passed of course). You never know who you're going to meet, especially at a gas station in Mississippi!

The daughters of the family I met at the gas station, proud to be holding their new egg shakers! :)

BIRTHPLACE OF THE BLUES

========================

Ah, the blues. I have always felt a calling toward this genre more than any other type of music. Lo and behold, as I pulled into Mississippi I realized that I was in the birthplace of it all! It was here that I discovered how and where the blues began, how it spread, and what blues music still stands for today! Thank you to the owners of The Mississippi Music Museum in Hazlehurst, Mississippi. They went out of their way to answer any and all questions I had. I must have been there for 3 hours.

B.B. KING

=============

Riley B. King earned his nickname, "B.B.," during his time as a disc jockey in Memphis where he was known as the "Beale Street Blues Boy." Years later, he became well-known as the most famous and recognized blues performer, becoming a bridge for black and white people of that time to come together and listen to the same type of music. It was one of the first times in mainstream music where this had happened! B.B. King was such a jovial and personable character and he was the perfect man for the job!

"No black. No white. Just the blues."

Let's hit the road B.B.!

"IT AIN'T FOOD IF IT AIN'T FRIED"!

==============================

Some of my favorite memories of Mississippi revolve around the food. I enjoyed ordering things like rutabagas, corn bread, collard greens, and early peas. The hospitality and food were not the only highlights however - it was the way they embraced their lifestyle as a whole!

A story I will never forget was when I stopped to get gas just south of Jackson, Mississippi. Much of the time, the only food available to me on the road was at gas stations. When I walked in, I noticed a large see-through case of fried food. I recognized the fried chicken, but didn't recognize anything else. I asked the woman at the register, "What is that?" as I pointed to the third and fourth thing I saw, trying not to be rude but curious. "That's fried jicama, and fried pickles." she answered. "And there?" I asked her as I pointed to the next window. "Fried cheese curds." she said. She now stopped what she was doing because she could tell she had an abnormal customer on her hands. I asked as nicely as I could, "Is there anything here that ISN'T fried?"

Right then, the woman that had been standing at the large fryer behind her looked over her shoulder at me and said, "Might be bad for the body, but it sure is good for the soul!"

I nodded my head, laughed with them, and ordered 4 items including fried mac & cheese. When in Rome...

March 12, 2019

Batson Children's Hospital

Jackson, Mississippi

Wow. What a morning. Walking into a room packed full of children sitting in a full circle. There were a variety of ages and reasons for each of them being there, and we all sang and played the egg shakers together to every song as if none of their differences mattered. Before leaving, I leaned over to one of the little girls and told her I was going to miss singing with her. Her response I will never forget, "We might be apart, but you will always be in my heart."

Thank you to the amazing staff here. Their energy and positive enthusiasm was infectious. Cutest part was bringing a group of nurses out to see the Jambulance. (QR code video below) says it all. I'm going to miss Mississippi. "BYE Y'ALL!!"

#byey'all #jambulance #musicismedicinetour

#37 ARKANSAS

LITTLE ROCK 9

=================

I had seen documentary footage and YouTube clips in the past about Central High School and the "Little Rock 9." Having been a school teacher myself, I was intrigued and wanted to learn more about segregation in schools during the 50's and 60's. I decided to visit Central High School, once a "whites only" school and the location of a huge civil rights turning point in 1957. I sat outside and watched as school got out. Seeing students of all races and ethnicities walk out together was a beautiful site to see, especially at such an impactful and historical location such as this.

WHY NOT ?

===========

On the tour, it was beautiful to see hospitals go out of their way to make their treatment center a place that was not only comfortable, but noticeably constructed and colorful for kids' needs. It got me thinking... What if they made normal 'adult' hospitals a little more fun and colorful as well? We could all use some more laughter and childlike innocence in our lives, especially in times of need.

March 15, 2019

Arkansas Children's Hospital

Little Rock, Arkansas

Congrats to Arkansas Children's Hospital, whose lobby and outdoor play area for children made for one of the most playful and positive environments I have witnessed in a hospital yet! Thank you for letting me add to the already present joy!!

#happyhospital #musicismedicine #musicismedicinetour

#38 TENNESSEE

BEALE STREET & ELVIS

===================

As I followed much of the blues trail up through Arkansas and into Tennessee, I knew I had to check out Beale Street, famous for its live music and atmosphere. It did not disappoint. It was also special for me to learn more about Elvis, walk through his house, and spend a day at the museum and in downtown Graceland. The southern hospitality, much like Elvis' charm, was once again in full effect. I seemed to make friends everywhere I went without any intention of doing so. ;)

NATIONAL CIVIL RIGHTS MUSEUM

============================

One of the most impressive museums and dedications I've ever seen was at the National Civil Rights Museum in Memphis and the location of Dr. Martin Luther King Jr.'s assassination. I was amazed to witness how many schools and children were walking through and learning. What an impact it must have each day on so many students and on anyone who visits. I had never seen so many materials, manuscripts, movies, and memorabilia together from one time in history. If there was ever a man deserving to have a museum dedicated in his name, it was Dr. Martin Luther King Jr.

March 18, 2019

Le Bonheur Children's Hospital

Memphis, Tennessee

Honestly, what attracted me to this particular hospital and made me want to play there, was the huge heart at the top of the roof! At night, it glows and shines down on the city as you drive by. :)

As I played music outside for families and children walking into the hospital, I noticed a child about 10 or 11 years old having a hard time walking inside. He was sitting in the middle of the sidewalk and was refusing anyone's help to stand up. You could tell he was scared. As I walked over to him, I started to play music softly. At first he didn't notice, but as I got closer his fear began to melt away. You could tell prior to being here, he had no correlation between the hospital and music being played. As he looked up, his hands raised toward his parents. As they started to help him to his feet, one of the security guards showed up with a balloon. The young child, his parents, the security guard and I, all walked into the hospital together to the sound of Bob Marley's, "Every little thing, is gonna be alright."

Thank you Le Bonheur for all you do for so many children. And thank you for letting me be a small part of it today.

#musicbringssmiles #lebonheurchildrenshospital

#musicismedicine

#39 MISSOURI

MY MOTHER'S ROOTS

==================

Learning about my family history has become so much more interesting to me as I've gotten older. I was able to visit the house and the resting place of my great-grandparents, as well as my grandma who had all passed before I was born. Calling my mom and my uncle to hear stories about their childhood, brought some laughs as well and even more interest in how far back my own family roots go!

March 24, 2019

Children's Mercy Adele Hall Campus

Kansas City, Missouri

The colors were so vibrant inside this hospital (shown below)! The signs outside, however, were my favorite part. They were on each of the street poles surrounding the hospital for blocks and blocks to greet those who were visiting. They each had messages of hope and of love with pictures of children, their mothers, and hospital staff.

#childrensmercy #colorfulhospital #musicismedicine

The colorful gift shop for pediatric patients as you walk into the hospital!

#40 KANSAS

THANKFUL PIT - STOP!

====================

Prior to showing up in Kansas, Joanna, whose family I played for in Florida, suggested I visit her and her boyfriend there. Thank God for her boyfriend, Forrest (pictured left). When I showed up to his house in Kansas City, he offered to give the Jambulance a much needed tune-up! He had worked on diesels for much of his life as a mechanic and saved me a lot of time and money. Luckily, he was able to see that the coolant overflow reservoir was cracked and that I was not going to be able to move on without getting a new one. We also replaced both headlights, put in a new battery, and filled all fluids. What a blessed pit stop!!

Joanna, Ian, and me before visiting Ruth in her room.

MY FIRST HEART TRANSPLANT EXPERIENCE

====================================

Both Joanna and Forrest welcomed me with open arms. Not only was my Jambulance back and healthy, Joanna had a friend whose mother Ruth (pictured right - opposite page), was in the hospital for a heart transplant. I was able to meet her as well as play music with Joanna for her at her bedside. Ruth is alive and well today, and with a new heart. What an incredible opportunity this was. Thank you again to Joanna and Forrest for their hospitality, and to Ian Bull for capturing such special moments!

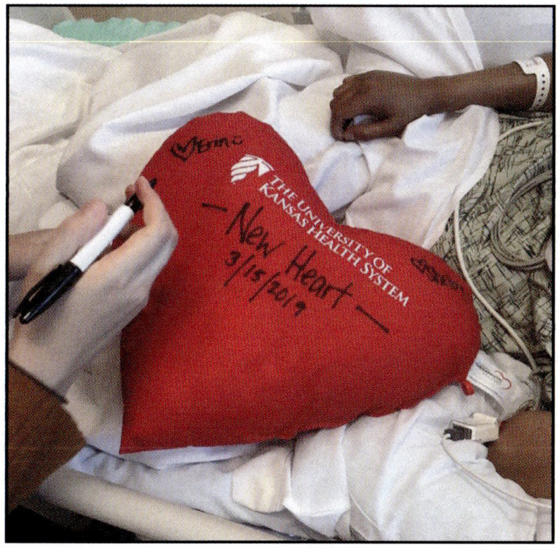

March 25, 2019

The University of Kansas Hospital -

Center for Advanced Heart Care

Kansas City, Kansas

Difficult to put into words what it's like to place your hand on the new beat of a heart that was just newly transplanted into someone. This brave woman was happier than anyone else in the room. Regardless of the pain she was experiencing, she sang and drummed away on her "new heart" pillow to a song she came up with herself!

You're an inspiration to us all Ruth. I will never forget singing with you. Thank you to all involved for allowing me to meet such an amazing woman and be part of such an amazing experience!

#newheart #idliketosingyouasong #musicismedicine

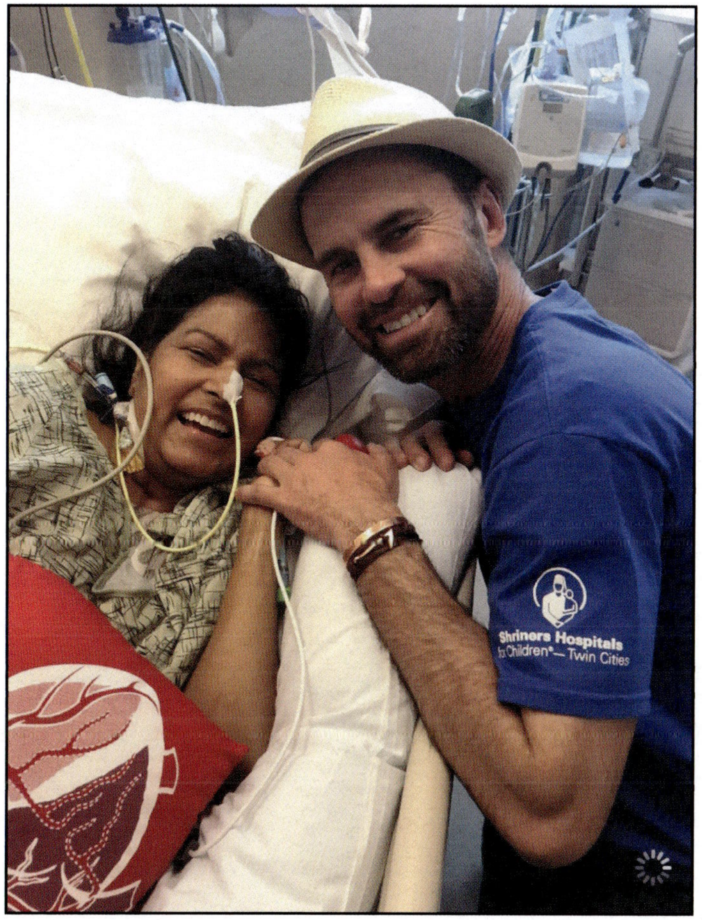

#41 OKLAHOMA

LAND RUN OF 1889

====================

What a crazy time. Can you imagine lining up with thousands of other people at a starting line to claim land?! Wagons, horse drawn carriages, you name it.. First come, first served!! April 22, 1889, people came from all over the country into the region of central Oklahoma known as the Unassigned Lands. According to the Homestead Act of 1862, if a settler could stay on the land they claimed for five years and improve it, the land would be theirs! (Oklahoma Historical Society)

FUN FACT: Why are they called the Oklahoma Sooners?? "Sooner," was the name given to anyone who entered the Unassigned Lands to claim land (too soon) before the official start date of the Land Run on April 22, 1889.

March 27, 2019

St. John Medical Center

Tulsa, Oklahoma

One of my favorite parts of this tour has been to visit hospitals across the country where different friends and family were born. Today, I visited and played music in the hospital where the only person I know from Oklahoma was born. Pierce Bryce, this one's for you!

St. John Medical Center was one of the first hospitals built in the state and beautifully kept. I played for patients and family members as they entered the hospital and waited in the lobby. The hospital had a certain charm to it and I felt like I could have stayed and played there for the entire day!

#stjohnshospital #musicismedicinetour

#42 TEXAS

March 29, 2019

Cook Children's Hospital

Fort Worth, Texas

What an impressive place. Inside the hospital included kid's shops, food markets, open ceilings, a recording studio, and its own news channel! I showed up at 10 am and left at 4 pm. I was blessed to be asked to play music for an event they were having today called, "The Day of the Doctor." The event entailed honoring doctors, their patients, and their families by pouring slime on the doctors' heads! Sitting in chairs in front of everyone, buckets were emptied from above, Nickelodeon-style! Much laughter, joy, and celebration were felt today throughout the entire Cook Children's campus.

I wouldn't have chosen to spend my day any differently. Thank you to Rayne, Abel, Raymond, and the entire staff for welcoming me to be a part!

#slimeismedicine #cookchildrens #dayofthedoctor #musicismedicinetour

RODEO CHAMPIONSHIP

========================

After ending my day at Cook Children's Hospital, someone told me there was a rodeo night in Fort Worth. It was starting soon and it happened to be the championships. So, 20 minutes later, I had a ticket to the rodeo right around the corner from where I was :) What a treat, getting to watch my first true Texas Rodeo, especially after such a long, rewarding day.

LONGEST DRIVE OF THE TOUR

===============================

It was now time to charge! This would be the longest drive of the tour (pictured right), as I would drive nearly 1/4 of the way across the country! It would also bring with it some sadness, as I was coming to terms that the tour was nearing completion. Only 9 more states to go!

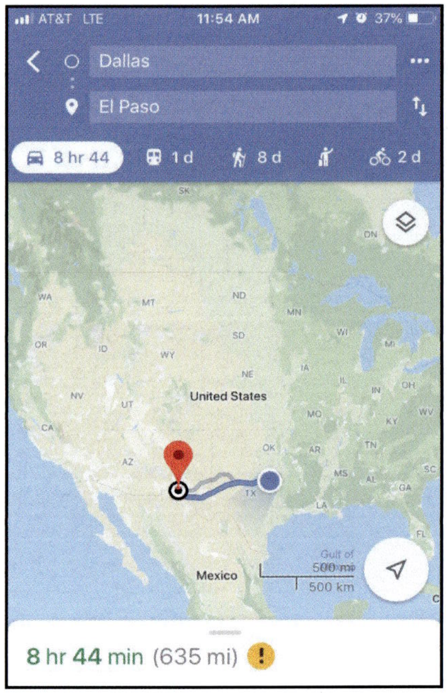

#43 NEW MEXICO

4 CORNERS

===============

As the tour continued, I found myself looking forward to the 4 corner states. It was of course the warmest part of the country this time of year. I could sense it as a reward toward the end of the tour to celebrate the accomplishment of visiting every state in the continental U.S. A final chapter of warmth and relaxation before finishing in Alaska and Hawaii!

WHITE SANDS, SANTA FE, & TAOS

================================

White Sands was beautiful. Such an open, unique setting of desert. In Sante Fe and Taos, you could feel a deep sense of history and presence of the Native American culture. Art was on display everywhere, and the desert and the color of the rocks and mountains were gorgeous!

April 4, 2019

Santa Fe Veterans Center

Santa Fe, New Mexico

To try and thank gentlemen such as these and to put into words my appreciation for their service would be impossible. Not only could words never represent such feelings, I have also never gone to war. I didn't fight in Vietnam and I will never be able to stand in such shoes as these. So, I did the only thing I knew to do. I asked them if they wanted to hear some music!

To see these men with tears in their eyes, bobbing their heads and laughing at the lyrics to songs they remembered from Vietnam was something I will never forget. This is a gift that only music can give.

"Just play us something that makes us feel gooood," one of the gentlemen requested.

I finished the day playing 3 Jimmy Buffett songs. They all laughed, and admitted they were all "Parrot Heads."

"I've never listened to a Jimmy Buffett song and not felt better afterwards. Ever!" one of them said with a grin. They all agreed with him and laughed. This laughter, through all that they have endured, was worth any amount of small sacrifice I could give myself.

Thank you gentlemen for your service. And thank you Santa Fe Veterans Center for having me. I respect and admire you all very much. I am honored to have been in your presence.

#thankyouforyourservice #vietnamvet

#musicismedicine

ANGEL FIRE

==============

I want to thank Greg Nichols. Greg was my high school football coach and is one of my family's dearest friends. He is the reason I visited the Angel Fire Vietnam Memorial, and is also my inspiration for visiting my first veterans center to play music. One of the more special parts of the tour was surprising Greg with a FaceTime call as I was at the Memorial. Veterans have donated bricks to honor their years of service, and I went there specifically to find Greg's. This is where Greg hopes someday to be laid to rest.

#44 COLORADO

A SECOND HOME

==================

The Rocky Mountains were spectacular. It was so awesome driving around in what seemed to be the base of them the entire time. From Boulder, downtown Denver, Evergreen, and the Red Rocks Amphitheatre, it felt like home. I hadn't realized so many people I had grown up with in Lake Tahoe had moved there and now I see why!

WHOOPS!

============

One of the more embarrassing stories of the tour, was when I accidentally slept in the parking lot of the facility (pictured left) where I was going to be playing the next day! I had no idea. In my defense, it didn't necessarily look like a traditional senior living facility. Turns out, in the past it was used for business offices, so there is (some) validity as to how I could do such a thing.

Yes, after playing and having one of the best times I have had on tour with seniors, I admitted and told the entire staff the story. We all laughed hysterically. Apparently (and before I awoke), several of the staff were asking why there was an ambulance parked in the parking lot in the morning and if there was an emergency!

April 9, 2019

The Center At Lincoln

Parker, Colorado

Still shaking my head. Imagine 10-12 seniors in walkers, following me with my guitar in single file, singing and marching around an entire rehab room. One by one, the staff would help them to their feet and each would join the marching band. Other exercises included step-ups, partner high-fives, roll the overgrown dice, and beach ball deflection. All the while, I was playing music in the background. I said numerous times I felt like we were in a music video. We all agreed. It was as if we had planned and practiced this for months! Laughter, egg shaking, dancing... All with assisted walkers!

Joy, Jen, and to all the physical therapy staff at The Center At Lincoln - you ladies are awesome. Your energy, innovative activities, and desire to connect with your patients was a sight to see. I'm looking forward to coming back here someday!! Thank you also to Marissa Braun for making this possible!

P.S. Thank you for the push-ups!! The staff invited me to join, as the residents rolled dice to see how many push-ups we had to do!

#musicismedicine #marchingband #dogoodfeelgood

#45 WYOMING

GRAND TETONS!!

=================

Wyoming is one state where I definitely wished I could have spent more time. I had been to Jackson Hole as a child, so to fast forward 30 years and be at the base of the Grand Tetons again was a treat! It felt like I was floating down a river through one of the most beautiful landscapes and meadows I had ever seen. At the end, was the most adorable country mountain town nestled right at the base of a ski area - Jackson Hole.

THE WALLACE FAMILY

====================

Thank you to Jim and Lemore Wallace. Jim was a college friend of my dad's and I stayed at their house for the night. After sharing some memories and stories, Jim suggested that I play at the St. John's Medical Center in Jackson, Wyoming.

April 11, 2019

St. John's Medical Center

Jackson, Wyoming

What a cute facility - very small and intimate. There were two different parts to the medical center, and I was asked to play in the lobby and the cafeteria for the senior living wing. My favorite part was being approached by a couple of the residents as they were eating lunch. They asked if I could come back and play every week. I smiled, gave them each a hug, and told them I'd definitely be back someday!

#stjohns #lunchtimejoy #musicismedicine

WATCHED AFTER

===================

I have included the picture I took above because it represents how I felt most of the tour. As if someone or something was looking out for me the entire time. To have decided to leave California in September and travel clock-wise through the northern states first, was against all odds. The fact that I made it through all 50 states without 4-wheel drive and never purchasing chains, says enough. I'm not suggesting anyone do the same, however, I do encourage us all to follow our gut and that 'little voice' inside. This voice is our connection to the greater whole and there is no better guide to lead the way. Thank you to the powers that be for looking out for me as the hawk that flew into the picture (above), represents.

FLYING BACK TO NEW JERSEY!!

===========================

Before visiting any hospitals in Utah, I was invited to Spotswood, New Jersey, to a drama production by a 5th grade class and their teacher, my new friend, Mayor Chris Slavicek. Since leaving New Jersey 4 months prior, I had been FaceTiming and meeting with the students over the phone, all leading up to the premiere of their upcoming play, Mary Poppins. The Music Is Medicine Tour was to be the recipient of their first *Give Back Campaign*! (Article below)

To read article, scan QR Code
description below.

(Clock-wise from top right) A picture of the students and me FaceTiming from the road. Chris, their teacher, proudly holding the board when they first started the fundraiser. The red buckets that the students used to raise money. And the board the students used to keep track of the money raised!

April 15, 2019

Appleby Elementary School

Spotswood, New Jersey

One of the main intentions of this tour is to give love and be of service to others. This weekend's trip to New Jersey, however, was a lesson in learning how to receive. To have the tour come back around in such a full circle as it did Saturday night, was something I could only stand witness to. Chris Slavicek and what he has done with these children, this community, and the Music Is Medicine Tour is something that will never be forgotten by all that were a part. Chris saw an opportunity to join forces, and took it. He gave these children a tangible example of how to give back to others, as they raised $8,000 for the Music Is Medicine Tour! Having FaceTimed and spoken with these children several times over the last couple of months, we formed relationships and consistent inspiration for each other, as I felt I had an additional healing team on the other side of the continent. I often referred to them as my "Music Is Medicine Tour & 1/2"!

To the Spotswood community, thank you for taking me in and welcoming me as one of your own, as well as for the generosity of your donations. To the students and Mary Poppins performers of the Appleby Elementary School, I already miss you. You have once again reminded me that my life is meant to be spent with children. Watching you all light up the stage tonight, was a reminder of the innocence and contagious zest for life that children consistently exude. And to Chris Slavicek, may this only be the beginning of our partnership. I have rarely ever witnessed such passion and commitment to something someone has put their mind and heart into. I would be honored to be a part of anything you choose to do in the future and am inviting myself back for your 20th year anniversary of this production!!

What a culminating event. What a reason to park the Jambulance and fly across the country! And what an example of how, "ANYTHING CAN HAPPEN IF YOU LET IT!"

- Mary Poppins

#spoonfullofsugar #applebyelementaryschool #marypoppins #musicismedicine

(Above) A picture of Chris and his 5th grade drama students holding the check for $8,000 raised for the tour! (Left) An unforgettable surprise at the end of the show from Chris, his students, and the community of Spotswood.

#46 UTAH

(BACK FROM NEW JERSEY) - PARK CITY

==================================

Thank you to Heather Currie, who the moment I arrived took me on a perfect tour through Park City, Utah. What an amazing ski town. It was like a large, Universal Studios set. Colorful houses, large snowflakes, and a hip movie/music scene.

MORMON TEMPLE, SALT LAKE CITY

==============================

I got to see the Mormon Central Temple, in Salt Lake City. It was absolutely gorgeous and was breathtaking to be around. With the white capped mountains in the distance, both the temple and the city looked as if they were glowing.

SPEECHLESS

============

How many pictures can I possibly take? I'd be driving, and it became unsafe how many times I would stop and try to take photos of the scenery through my windows. I remember thinking at least 30 times, I've never seen something so beautiful! Moab Arches, Bryce Canyon, Zion National Park - it was just a huge postcard! This is a bold statement and part of me hates to say it, but Utah, you are the most gorgeous state I have ever seen.

April 19, 2019

Primary Children's Hospital - Salt Lake City, Utah

Provo Canyon School - Springville, Utah

What an honor yesterday, to have been able to visit and play music for 2 different places. The first was Primary Children's Hospital in Salt Lake City, Utah. Once again, I am reminded of how simple and impactful handing out an egg shaker to a child can be. Anything to take their mind off of the reason they might be here. Playing music for them is one thing, but handing them something they can always use to create music for themselves...? Priceless.

Second, I drove from Salt Lake City to Provo, Utah, where I was invited to speak and play music for students. What a unique experience, not only to be able to connect with children in a school setting, but to be invited by the Executive Director who used to coach football with my father in Lake Tahoe 30 years ago.

Provo Canyon School, an intensive, psychiatric youth residential treatment center, was the first of its kind that I've visited on the tour. I was able to share stories with the students, funny things that have happened, lessons I have learned on the road, and hardships I have encountered. I also answered any questions they had about all of it! My favorite part, however, was in the middle of the last song we sang together. I stopped playing. Aside from all the mental stresses or worries each of them were facing in their own lives, I pointed out that there wasn't one person in the room who wasn't playing their instrument, or singing, or smiling. Not one.

They all laughed, and we finished playing the last song together!

Dave and Kathy Hampton, you two are amazing with the amount of love and resources you offer to these children and students. I thank you for the invitation and for allowing me to be a small part of all of your lives for an afternoon. May the laughter and joy that was shared yesterday be a reminder to us all that the desire to smile never dies in anyone. Especially those most in need.

I look forward to the day I come back and see you all once again.

#provocanyonschool #dogoodfeelgood

#musicismedicine

Intermountain
Primary Children's
Medical Center
The Child First and Always®

#47 ARIZONA

FINALLY WARM ENOUGH!

=====================

When the tour started, I had hoped to do some camping. Unfortunately, due to the cold, I wasn't able to until now! 47 states in, and I was finally able to sleep with the doors open, unzip my sleeping bag, and enjoy the outdoors at night (bottom left)! Lake Havasu, thank you!

SEDONA, GRAND CANYON

=====================

The Grand Canyon was closed, due to snow. Sedona, however, was one of the more beautiful places I had ever been. I had been there once in the past, but the color of the rocks and overall peace one receives when visiting there is something I will never forget.

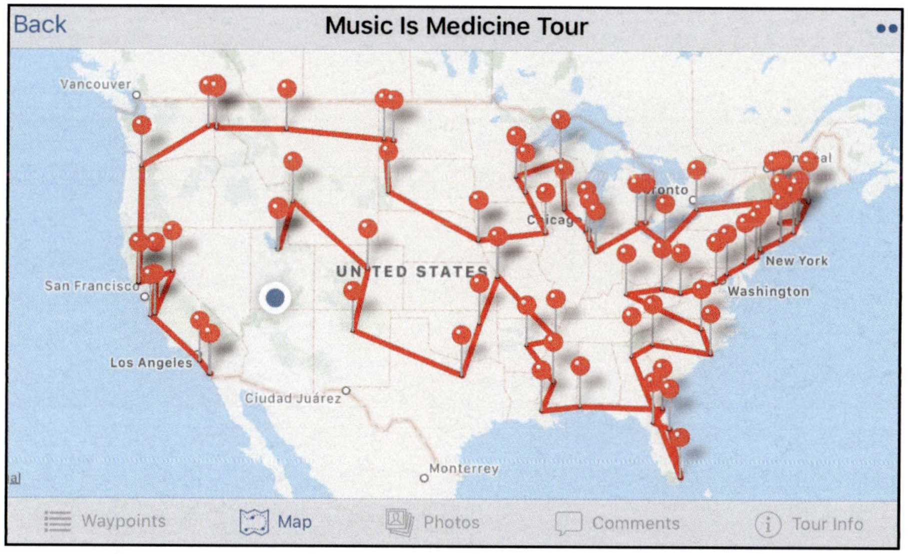

April 26, 2019

HonorHealth Thomas Peak Medical Center

Scottsdale, Arizona

First off, I want to thank "SeaSpine," a medical device company that provides spine surgery instruments and implants for doctors and their patients. Having been through surgery myself to have a spinal tumor removed, I felt connected to their vision. Based out of San Diego, California, they have been supportive the entire way throughout the Music Is Medicine Tour. Thank you especially to Kelly Lenzkes. Without her introducing us, none of this would have happened today!

Picture an entire office lobby filled with nearly every employee in the hospital circled up for their "Weekly Huddle," as they call it. The weekly meetings normally consist of company updates, any changes that need to made, etc. Well, today the "huddle" consisted of music as medicine with egg shakers and singing. Everyone was in a circle, laughing and taking part in song. Afterward, the facilitator said, "Alright! That's it! Have a great rest of your day!" Hugs and high-fives as people left - now THAT'S a company meeting!

Thank you to the Thomas Peak hospital crew for inviting me in, taking me to every floor to visit patients, and trusting me with your residents and co-workers the entire morning. Pretty special to hear music and see smiles spread throughout all of the hospital.

Lastly, a memorable birthday dedication once again to HOLLY (below). You're amazing, and it was no coincidence that we met and that this all transpired on your birthday. You deserved every second of it.

#honorhealth #bdaygirl #bethechange
#musicismedicine #musicismedicinetour

#48 NEVADA

April 27, 2019

Sunrise Children's Hospital

North Las Vegas, Nevada

Well, it was quite the eventful day yesterday. The morning was filled with music, and the afternoon/evening with AAA and coolant!

- MORNING - Sunrise Children's Hospital

Sometimes the music that is to be played in hospitals isn't necessarily meant only for the patients, but the family members and loved ones who are in support. Today, I stayed in the lobby of Sunrise Children's Hospital the entire time. I played music and talked with those waiting to hear news and who had visitation rights in the lobby. Feels good to know that everyone involved needs a little help and kindness, a little music, and a little hope where it might have been forgotten.

- AFTERNOON/EVENING - Roadside, AAA Auto Care

The first thought that crossed my mind as I sat on the curb in North Las Vegas was how thankful I was for the Jambulance. It had taken me over 24,000 miles and I had experienced no serious problems since putting in the new engine and starting this journey 8 months ago! Well, this afternoon there was a BOOM! Under the hood and in 98 degree heat, the coolant vent and shroud burst into pieces and punctured a hole in the radiator causing all coolant to empty to the ground. Six 1/2 hours

later, I was finally towed at 8pm to a local mechanic, slept in their parking lot in the Jambulance, and woke up to "face the music."

Best part of the day? Giving the tow truck driver's son, "Jr." an electric guitar. He and his dad had gone well out of their way not only to pick me up, but to take me to the best mechanic possible to ensure my being safe for the rest of the trip. "Jr." had been talking non-stop in the back seat about how he wanted to learn guitar. I knew exactly what I was to do with a gift that my friend Dan Dominguez had given me. Dan had asked me in Arizona to give the guitar to a child of my choice, and I knew this was the one. Just look at his smile!

Breakdown = Breakthrough

#breakdownequalsbreakthrough #giveyourgiftaway #musicismedicinetour

Jr. with his new guitar :)

COMING HOME!!

===============

How amazing it was to come home, and drive up and see my Mom & Pops standing on the front deck with a sign that read, "**WELCOME HOME, RYAN AND JAMBU!**" (picture bottom right :) Being home was perfect. I remember lying on the living room carpet, resting like never before! There was something extremely different about not having to be anywhere, not being by myself anymore, and being in a nice warm home. I was able to turn off for the first time since starting the tour and quickly realized this was exactly what I needed.

May 6, 2019

Lake Tahoe, California

Well, what a beautiful, short homecoming it was. I apologize to those I didn't update that I was home and safe after the minor breakdown in Las Vegas. It was time for me to rest, and get ready for the last 2 states of the tour!!

So perfect to spend time skiing with my Mama, working out with my Pops, and have them both stick the last guitar on the continental 48 map!! Thank you both so much Mom & Pops for the support from afar, and always providing such a loving, warm home to come back to.

May 1st was also Phil Carrillo's Birthday. He would have been 42 years old. It was so special that I got to be home and spend his birthday with his mom, both his sisters, step dad, and friends that love him so. Love you Flip!!

And love to all of you who celebrate days such as these, in both remembrance and acknowledgment of those who have passed. By doing so, they sustain such a presence in our lives today!!

As the "Lake Rules" say... Get back to nature, jump in the lake, and rest relax & reflect. These were all definitely done.

Here's to the last of all 50 states!! Alaska & Hawaii - HERE I COME!!

#family #Flip #home #musicismedicinetour

Both of my parents standing over their sign, "**WELCOME HOME, RYAN AND JAMBU!**"

#49 ALASKA

TO DRIVE OR NOT TO DRIVE

=========================

Originally when I had started the tour, I wanted to drive to Alaska. As the days moved on while in Tahoe, I soon realized that I just didn't have that same amount of energy and stamina as when I started the tour. There was very little phone reception in Alaska, I had heard the roads were not always well maintained, and I wasn't sure if AAA was as accessible as it is here in the lower 48. It had been close to 8 1/2 months and I was very proud of what I had done and what the tour had accomplished. Lastly, as I was home, it gave me the chance to imagine for a second... What if I just flew? How incredibly nice and warm did that sound?!

2 days later, Stephanie, a friend of mine who is an employee for United Airlines, reached out to me. She told me that she wanted to help the tour and offered me 2 standby tickets to Alaska and Hawaii! Well, sounds like the decision was made for me! I packed up 2 backpacks - 1 full of egg shakers and the other with clothes. I grabbed my guitar of course, and I was off! Oh yah, one small add-on.. Stephanie surprised me with my first ever, FIRST CLASS TICKET! Thank you again Steph!

OUT OF MY ELEMENT

======================

It took some adjusting when I first landed in Fairbanks, Alaska. I had never been without the Jambulance this entire tour. Should I catch a cab to a hotel? Should I rent a car, then go to a hotel? After mulling over all the different options, I decided that renting a car would not only give me the freedom to travel and drive where I wanted, but I could also save money and sleep in it! It was pretty amusing watching me in the car lot look for the car I wanted. I would put the seats down in each car I was interested in and lie down in the back, making sure it had enough room in it for me to sleep. It definitely turned some heads from others at the airport.

I ended up choosing to rent a Subaru Outback. It had 4-wheel drive, room to lay down comfortably, and decent gas mileage. I had found my new (temporary) Alaskan home!

ONE GIANT NATIONAL PARK

========================

Alaska was like driving through one gigantic National Park. I think they said 80% of the state is not accessible by traditional road or vehicle. You have to either hike, mush, (be pulled by sled and dogs) or snowmobile in! A "scratch my head moment," was when I kept seeing extension cords hanging out the front grill of everyone's radiator. I had never seen this before and having grown up in the snow, was surprised by such a thing. Apparently, when the temperature gets below zero, plugging in the battery helps the vehicle start as well as keeps the battery warm overnight. This would explain why in the parking lots, there were outlets sticking up out of the ground for you to plug into at each parking spot! Luckily it was spring so I didn't have to experience this!

DENALI, TALKEETNA & CHENA HOT SPRINGS

======================================

Denali National Park was beautiful, Talkeetna was my favorite small town, and Chena Hot Springs was my spot to get warm and relax. I got to visit a couple of places where they keep professional sled dogs, and also ran into several groups of people preparing for their next big mountain ascent. My favorite part, however, was how long it stayed light outside! I love the sun and have no problem sleeping in light, so my long days were golden!

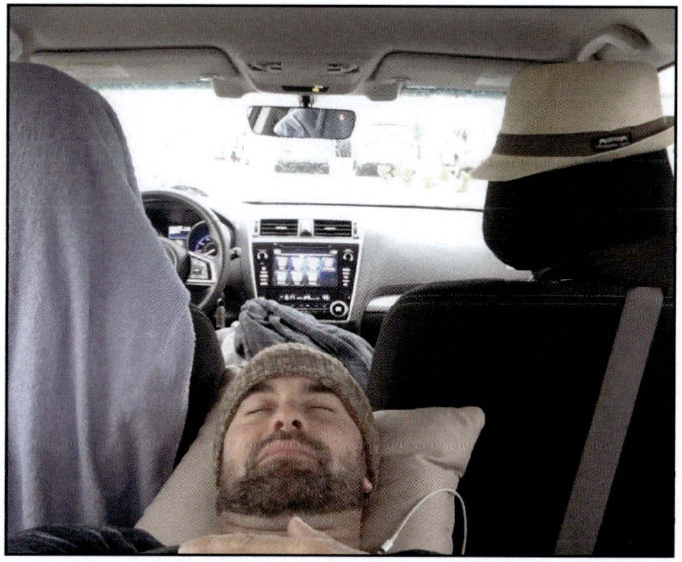

Lying down to sleep at 1 am, light as day!

ALASKA NATIVE MEDICAL CENTER

May 9, 2019

Alaska Native Medical Center

Anchorage, Alaska

First of all, Happy MOTHER'S DAY!! To all the mothers out there, especially my own, there isn't a day that goes by that your unconditional love isn't felt and known. My mom and I have only become closer since the time I left, and for this, I am thankful.

Secondly, Happy NURSES WEEK!! From the time of my own tumor surgery and through every day on this tour, my appreciation and humility only grows toward these givers. I tell nurses in every hospital I visit, "I come in here for a couple hours, play a few songs and I'm gone. You guys are the ones in here DAY-in & DAY-out, doing what you do and caring for people. Thank you, thank you, thank you!"

Brett Brolliar & Kelsey Brolliar *(2 of the best ;)*

Well, what an absolute gift Alaska has been. Thank you especially to Roberta Miljure and Darbi Daley, for being living examples of the love and the soul that the indigenous people of this state share. When searching for a hospital where I could play, I was attracted to the name, "Alaska Native Medical Center." I was hoping that I could meet and play for the natives of this land, and also learn as much as I could about their traditions, ways of life, and their health care system. It turned out to be the perfect place.

Roberta, thank you for the gifts, for welcoming me, and for the passion you exude for the hospital and it's people. Darbi, thank you for spending such a large part of the day with me. Any question I asked, you would get more and more excited to share your answers. My favorite part of the day was when you asked me if I would come and play for your grandpa (below). Roberta and Darbi, you are the epitome of serving, passion, and living your purpose in the workplace. You both facilitated the exact experience this tour was created upon. Thank you also to Michael Doyle for capturing such moments of joy on camera throughout the morning. Goodbye Alaska. Until next time!

#musicismedicine #alaskanativemedicalcenter

#50 HAWAII

THE PERFECT END TO A PERFECT JOURNEY

====================================

What better way to end the tour than in Hawaii. I ended up staying for 7 days, which was 3 days longer than any other state. I was so excited to be warm each day and especially to sleep outside! I decided to rent a truck and planned to lay down the tailgate, slip into a sleeping bag each night, and sleep under the stars.

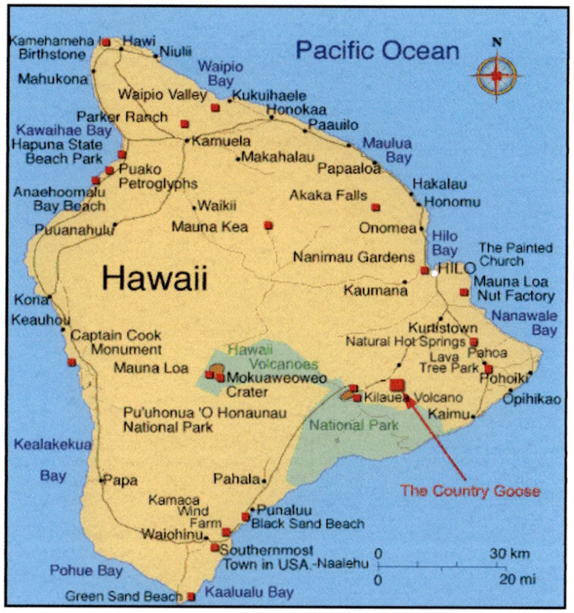

The first night, after I had just finished setting up my sleeping arrangement, it started to pour. Yep, tropical rain. I had completely forgotten, and lay there laughing as I was soaked within the first 30 seconds. Needless to say, I never set the bed up in the back again. For the next week, I slept in the rear cab with my feet outstretched over the dashboard and steering wheel in the front. Not the most comfortable, but I made it work. After all, I was on my 50th state, and no minor discomfort was going to stop me now!

What a beautiful island. Of the Hawaiian islands I've visited, I have to say, the Big Island is my favorite. The most amount of land with the least amount of people. I managed to drive around the entire island, eat more mangoes than I ever have, and gain a greater understanding of the meaning, "Aloha." My favorite Aloha definition - "to share the breath of life."

Well Hawaii, you sure shared your breath of life with me. I've never felt so in tune with the land and its abundance as I did while spending a week with you and your people. "ALO-HA!!"

SMALL TOWN FEEL

==================

When I drove into the town of Honokaa the night before I was scheduled to play, there happened to be a town parade, talent show, and market down the entire middle of the street! So perfect.
This small town made me feel like I was home.

May 19, 2019
Hale Ho'ola Hamakua Hospital
Honokaa, Hawaii

I don't think I could have asked for a better "last hospital experience" to represent the end of this 9 month tour. Thank you to the staff, the patients, and the beautiful small town of Honokaa for taking me in! To be honest, it was a rather emotional day. When I arrived, the staff gifted me with a lei made of wood and leaves. Unexpectedly, it brought me to tears. I realized in that moment that this was the last hospital stop. The last of this amazing tour and journey.

The staff there made me a sign, had a microphone and seat set up for me, and an entire room filled with happy, music-hungry residents! The Jambulance might not have been there, but the participation of the residents and staff to place the last of the "50 state stickers" on the guitar case was a beautiful substitute!

Thank you especially to Natalie and Fallon, who made this tour stop happen. Fallon, who called me from her cell phone to politely coerce me into coming Sunday, was one of several other staff members who came in on their day off to be a part of the Music Is Medicine festivities. This won my heart over.

Mahalo to all of you! And may we all learn from the Hawaiian islands, to invite more "Aloha Love" into each of our lives!

#aloha #50hospitals50states #musicismedicine #musicismedicinetour

May 20, 2019

Kailua-Kona, Hawaii

We did it!! ALL 50!! Thank you to all of you. I could not have done it without all of your support!

Here's to a sun-filled, proud, humbled man. 50+ hospitals/50 states. Couldn't have done it without all of you and your kind words and support the entire way. Tonight I am letting go and saying goodbye to a journey that will be a part of me forever. More importantly, a part of all the people the tour touched.

Cheers everyone. Here's to being of service and living out your purpose!

#musicismedicinetour #50hospitals50states #cheers!!

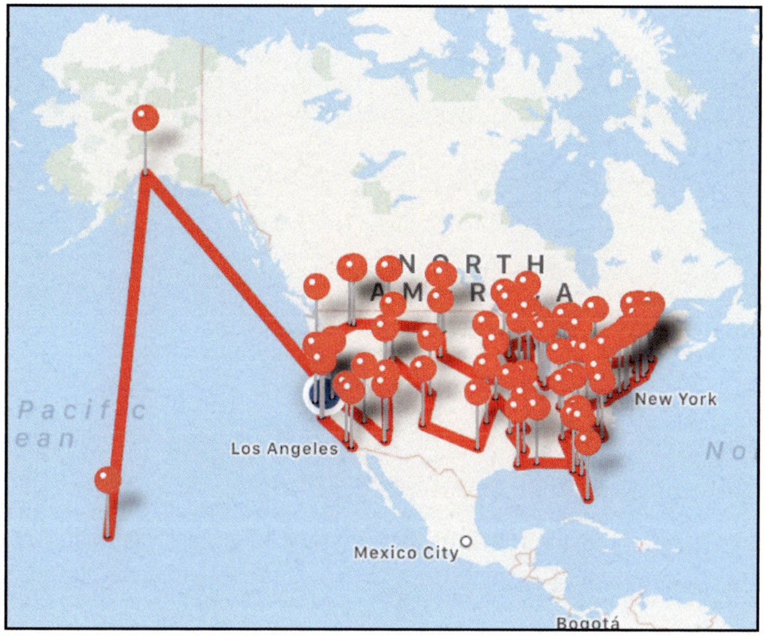

A FINAL MESSAGE

================

If I could lend one last gift or lesson that I learned from this entire journey, it was the fulfillment, joy, and peace that being of service brought to me. I believe one's own self to be half until given wholly to help another. I have told several people and it might sound strange to say... I could die today and be at peace.

I realize this is a bold statement. I also realize how good it feels when I say it. To have strived my entire life to try to "*be somebody*," I seemed to have "*found myself*" in being of service to others. I always thought it was the other way around. I thought that in order to be happy and find purpose and fulfillment, that I would need to accomplish my goals and dreams and be #1 in something. Well, if I could share the most important lesson now, it is to be #1 in someone else's life! Whether this be as a father, a mother, a teacher, or a nurse, those of you who have experienced this selfless fulfillment know that there are very few things greater.

You see, here's the secret - I feel to be happiest in life, one needs to do two things:

1. Find and follow your passion and the truest expression of who you are.
2. Use it to help your fellow man/woman. It's really that simple.

Don't know your passion? Lose yourself in service, and your passion will find you. Know your passion but don't know how to use it? Use it to help another. Don't worry about the money, it will come. And if it doesn't, you're not trusting the service you're providing. If you are making the world a better place, the world will make you better for it.

I feel blessed to have been able to find my passion in music. And I have never felt more fulfilled in all the years of playing music as when I played for a young girl who needed it most. I also knew in that moment, that there would never be anything else more gratifying to do with my life. It was simple - either use the gift I was given to play music for people in need, or live an unfulfilled life. As if I had been given an assignment that if I didn't live out, I'd be ignoring my destiny and the reason I am here.

Thank you all for taking the time to read this book and share in the journey. Thank you also for doing your part in helping each other in your own, unique ways. I leave you with a quote from Pablo Picasso...

"The meaning of life is to find your gift.
The purpose of life is to give it away."

A final QR Code video in closing memory and appreciation.

MUSIC IS MEDICINE TOUR

The final map on the inside wall of the Jambulance! It's pretty amazing to see. I used this map the entire trip to plot all stops (with red yarn & white stickies) from start to finish. The "Jambulance Headquarters" I often referred to it as ;) It also includes places I stayed, sites I visited, and every hospital stop on the tour. Don't forget about Alaska and Hawaii on the bottom left!

THANK YOU TO ALL HOSPITALS & LOCATIONS!! (78)

(In the order visited)

==

* **Rady Children's Hospital** - San Diego, California
* **Community Hospital of the Monterey Peninsula** - Monterey, California
* **Witter Ranch Elementary School** - Sacramento, California
* **Tahoe Forest Extended Care** - Truckee, California
* **Healdsburg Senior Living Community** - Healdsburg, California
* **Doernbecher Children's Hospital** - Portland, Oregon
* **Shriners Hospital for Children** - Spokane, Washington
* **Kootenai Health** - Coeur d'Alene, Idaho
* **Rehabilitation Hospital of the Northwest** - Coeur d'Alene, Idaho
* **Benefis Health System** - Great Falls, Montana
* **CHI St. Alexis Health** - Dickinson, North Dakota
* **Rapid City Regional Health** - Rapid City, South Dakota
* **Boys Town National Research Hospital** - Boys Town, Nebraska
* **University of Iowa Stead Family Children's Hospital & Clinics** - Iowa City, Iowa
* **Mayo Clinic** - Rochester, Minnesota
* **Shriners Hospital for Children** - Twin Cities, Minnesota
* **UW Health University Hospital** - Madison, Wisconsin
* **Home Visit, "Team Scotty"** - Pleasanton, California

* **Home Visit, Grandpa Bill** - Evanston, Illinois
* **Cedar Creek Assisted Living** - Lowell Indiana
* **Home Visit, "Team Peyton"** - Lowell Indiana
* **Gold Star Cafe** - Lowell Indiana
* **C.S. Mott Children's Hospital** - Ann Arbor, Michigan
* **Akron Children's Hospital** - Akron, Ohio
* **The Pines at Rutland Center for Nursing and Rehabilitation** - Rutland, Vermont
* **Dartmouth Hitchcock Medical Center** - Lebanon, New Hampshire
* **Ronald McDonald House** - Portland, Maine
* **Barbara Bush Children's Hospital** - Portland, Maine
* **Care Well Urgent Care** - Peabody, Massachusetts
* **Brigham & Women's Hospital** - Boston, Massachusetts
* **Hasbro Children's Hospital** - Providence, Rhode Island
* **Essex Meadows Senior Living** - Essex, Connecticut
* **Alive Inside & Brooks Brothers** - Madison Ave, New York City
* **The Brooklyn Hospital Center** - Brooklyn, New York

HOSPITALS CONTINUED ...

======================

* **Hospital of The University of Pennsylvania** - Philadelphia, Pennsylvania
* **Chelsea Senior Living** - Helmetta, New Jersey
* **Kent General** - Dover, Delaware
* **Milford Memorial** - Dover, Delaware
* **A.I. DuPont Nemours Children's Hospital** - Dover, Delaware
* **The Johns Hopkins Hospital** - Baltimore, Maryland
* **Birmingham Green Health Care** - Manassas, Virginia
* **Gesundheit Institute** - Hillsboro, West Virginia
* **University of Kentucky Health Care** - Lexington, Kentucky
* **Duke Raleigh Hospital** - Raleigh, North Carolina
* **Shriners Hospital for Children** - Greenville, South Carolina
* **Annandale Village** - Suwanee, Georgia
* **Home Visit** - Jacksonville, Florida
* **Home Visit** - Hilliard, Florida
* **UF Health Cancer Hospital** - Gainesville, Florida
* **Coastal Church** - Daytona Beach, Florida
* **Home Visit** - Miami, Florida
* **USA Children & Women's Hospital** - Mobile, Alabama
* **Our Lady of the Lake Regional Medical Center** - Baton Rouge, Louisiana
* **Batson Children's Hospital** - Jackson, Mississippi
* **Arkansas Children's Hospital** - Little Rock, Arkansas
* **Le Bonheur Children's Hospital** - Memphis, Tennessee
* **Children's Mercy Adele Hall Campus** - Kansas City, Missouri
* **University of Kansas Hospital Center for Advanced Heart Care** - Kansas City, Kansas
* **St. John Medical Center** - Tulsa, Oklahoma
* **Cook Children's Hospital** - Fort Worth, Texas
* **Santa Fe Veterans Center** - Santa Fe, New Mexico
* **The Center At Lincoln** - Parker, Colorado
* **St. John's Health** - Jackson, Wyoming
* **Appleby Elementary School** - Spotswood, New Jersey
* **Primary Children's Hospital** - Salt Lake City, Utah
* **Provo Canyon School** - Springville, Utah
* **HonorHealth Thomas Peak Medical Center** - Scottsdale, Arizona
* **Sunrise Children's Hospital** - Las Vegas, Nevada
* **Alaska Native Medical Center** - Anchorage, Alaska
* **Hale Ho'ola Hamakua Hospital** - Honokaa, Hawaii

ACKNOWLEDGEMENTS

======================

I wanted to end this journey by thanking everyone that was along for the ride from the very beginning! Thank you to Stephanie Ousley, Linda Hutkin Slade, and Debbie Mason, who first opened their doors at Sharp Grossmont Hospital in San Diego to let me come and play for their patients. This is where it all began!

To the "Art & Chat" crew - Britta, you will always be an inspiration to me. Your unapologetic strength and positive attitude kept me going through much of this journey. Juliette, you will always be an angel on my shoulder. Your advice I will never forget.

Thank you to Forrest Casey, who not only provided me with his ambulance, but taught me from the ground up how to build and swing a hammer! Thank you also to the Casey family! - Robin, Dash, & Fin, who hosted me the entire summer while the build of the Jambulance happened!

Denny Luther - Thank you for your support from the very beginning. Your excitement helped validate for me that such an undertaking was not only possible, but needed.

Todd Murray - Your pace at which you work will always be a phenomenon to me. Thank you for your time and energy welding and building the Jambulance roof rack and kitchen table!

Derek and Casey at Wrap City in San Diego - Thank you for your wrapping of the Jambulance and making it so beautiful! He shined the entire way!

Wendi Williams - Your support from the very beginning of this journey will never be forgotten. I could not have done this without our many talks, planning, and much encouragement from you.

Ian - Amazing footage from the tour. Most of all, your passion for this project and the tour as a whole. I have yet to meet anyone who has the same amount of commitment as you to capture and bring out the best of an individual, their art, and it's intention.

Joanna - What a blessing to have met you. You are the best of facilitators, both of people and of their unique self-expression. There is nothing you can't do or learn to do, and you are one of the most intuitive people I have met. Thank you for your listening and commitment to this tour in the small and impactful window we had together.

Melissa & Dave - You both were responsible for keeping me warm!! Melissa, thank you for your advice and motivation and helping to get things organized and streamlined out of the gate! I knew you were there anytime I needed you and that you will continue to always be. Dave, you have quickly become a mentor to me. Your genuine leadership and enjoyment of life is something I will always strive to exemplify myself.

Kimmy - Without you, this book simply would not have been purchased in the timely fashion it was. May our support and friendship only continue to grow!

Kelly & SeaSpine - Thank you SeaSpine for not only inviting me to play at one of your hospitals, but most importantly for the support and continued work you do for so many! Thank you Kell, for always believing in and sharing the tour and it's story with so many at SeaSpine and beyond!

Lauren Merriman - Do you know how many children and seniors you helped bring smiles to?? Thousands of egg shakers that you were responsible for providing, are being used as we speak to bring music and joy to those in need. YOU! are responsible for the musical egg-shaking ripple effect! Forever!

Heidi - Our many talks not only kept me company on the road, but helped me to further my growth. I also appreciate your support and vision with the book. I am so thankful we are back in each other's lives and I know we will always be a stand for each other.

Gabe Rosenshine - Your fire for life my man, inpsires me and always inspired our boy, Philly. I am lucky to you have you in my corner, always.

Andy and Christian - Thank you for being an ear for me day in and day out and helping me to create my intention and focus anytime it was needed. I can't tell you how much my sanity and the success of the tour depended on such a listening from you both.

Nikki - From the time I met you, I knew you were an angel. You are stronger than most, and I want you to know I have always seen this in you. Thank you or our many talks. Your love, support, and courage will always be with me.

Chris Slavicek - You saw the potential of this tour from the first time we met. Thank you for joining the tour with your students, the support from your entire community, and the continued stand you are for me today. YOU were the one who put your foot down and who told me to write this darn thing!!

To my proofreading/editing/brainstorming book peeps - Kenn Pride, Forrest Casey, Michelle Hu, Dan Swint, JudeSuzeDeb, BC, Andy Bayon, Sat Hari, my Mama, and my Bro ...

Pride - From the get-go, you have been in my corner talking me through all my fears, helping me to set goals and weekly deadlines, and encouraging me to take one step at a time. I couldn't have done it without you pal.

Forrest/Pharoah - Your experienced yet simple approach to life has leaked over to yet another part of mine, this book. Thank you for always bringing humor and such a matter a fact way of looking at things to our conversations and friendship. You always keep my head straight by reminding me we are one laugh away from seeing the big picture.

Michelle - You have always "seen" me since the time we met. You will forever be a stand for my truth and an ear for my best. This book would have had many emberrasingg mistaykes if it werent' four you!! ;)

Swint - From Cherry Street until now, I have always enjoyed your wit. I am lucky to have been able to call on it as one of the last pair of eyes to read this book.

JudeSuze - You amaze me with your gusto. The pace at which you do things will always make me shake my head. May we always stand around the fire.

ACKNOWLEDGEMENTS CONTINUED...

================================

BC - My creative soulmate. From the time we met, we knew we would be collaborating for the long haul. I admire your passion and integrity, and appreciate you bringing it into the editing of this book. Here's to many more talks to come!

Andy - "Andy Bayon (writer) Masterminds". I'll never change it. About time I took advantage of this gift! You were the last eyes upon it!

Sat Hari - A soul that will be with mine always. How much more confidence it gave me knowing you were in my corner. Here's to always sharing, together.

Mama - An English teacher for life! May I always be grateful for your corrections of my speaking and grammar! Thank you for taking on the first edit of this book. Most of all, thank you for your patience.

Bro - Such a talented and intelligent dude. I am honored that I get to live this life with you as my brother. Thank you for your feedback and constant reflection throughout this entire process.

Michael and Tai at the Alive Inside Coalition - Thank you so much for what you do for the thousands of men and women with dementia, and for the thousands of children who you connect them with. Thank you for seeing the potential of this tour from the beginning and offering to partner with me in making it happen!

Justin Brunner - With me from start to finish, and that's exactly what you were responsible for. Building the foundation that the entire tour was built upon (GoFundMe video), to the end and the final touches (front and rear cover and build video). Couldn't have done this without you pal.

@shotbybrunner

Elvis - Shooting pics and vid, putting together the closing montage, and one of only two people to join me on the road. Your variety of talents and ability to learn and develop more as they come to you is incredible and admirable to watch. May this only be a sign of what is to come for us together.

@joshallenimages

Mom, Pops, Brother, Kelsey, and Lil' D! (Desa) - Thank you for always being my voice of reason. Thank you for supporting me no matter what new idea I come up with. Thank you for always making the time and keeping me in touch with the family and Desa on FaceTime while on the road! And thank you for helping this book get done in the timely fashion it did! Everything you do I know always comes from love and wanting the best for me. For this, I am forever grateful. I love you.

Lastly, I want to thank everyone who supported this amazing tour from afar. The donors from GoFundMe, the Facebook & Instagram support, and all those that took me in and hosted me along the way! I obviously couldn't have done it without each and every one of you. Your financial contributions, texts, emails, and thoughts/prayers were felt and received every single day. I said a few times on the journey that because of this, it felt like I was never alone. What an amazing feeling it was, to be a part of something so much bigger than myself and alongside all of you. Until we meet again, may we all continue to see the light, and be the light.

MUSIC IS MEDICINE.

ABOUT THE AUTHOR

=====================

Ryan Brolliar, a native of North Lake Tahoe, California, presently splits his time between the lake and San Diego, California. Time with his family, sharing his story, and playing music for those who need it most are where he is happiest. And of course (as pictured below), when he is with his Jambulance.

To find out any information about future tours, books, and locations where he will be speaking and playing, please visit: MusicisMedicineTour.com

MusicisMedicineTour.com